The
Hollywood
Sisters

on location

The Hollywood Sisters

backstage pass

on location

The Hollywood Sisters

on location

Mary Wilcox

DELACORTE PRESS

The author wishes to thank the brilliant teen readers at New London High School.

Published by Delacorte Press
an imprint of Random House Children's Books
a division of Random House, Inc.
New York

www.randomhouse.com/teens

Educators and librarians, for a variety of teaching tools, visit us at
www.randomhouse.com/teachers

Library of Congress Cataloging-in-Publication Data
Wilcox, Mary.
On location / Mary Wilcox.—1st ed.
p. cm. — (The Hollywood sisters)
Summary: Thirteen-year-old Jessica, a recovering shy girl and poet, continues her sleuthing on the set of her sister's television sitcom—this time to discover the prankster who is delaying the show's production.
ISBN: 978-0-385-73355-7 (trade pbk.) — ISBN: 978-0-385-90370-7 (lib. bdg.)
[1. Sisters—Fiction. 2. Actors and actresses—Fiction. 3. Television—Production and direction—Fiction. 4. Poetry—Fiction. 5. Hollywood (Los Angeles, Calif.)—Fiction. 6. Mystery and detective stories.] I. Title.
PZ7.W645680nl 2007
[Fic]—dc22   2006002317

Printed in the United States of America

10 9 8 7 6 5 4 3 2 1

First Edition

For my sister Julie Coll

Dear _TRL_ host and crew,
You're tops at what you do!
We were thrilled to see you decide
To put Eva on _TOTAL REQUEST LIVE._

The at~home interview
For the big MTV debut
Seemed like a brilliant notion.
That—oops!—ended in _Total_ commotion!

Looking back, at some future time,
We might find humor in the crime—
Perhaps cracking up like loons.
But that won't be anytime soon.

HERE ARE FIVE THINGS YOU NEED TO KNOW WHEN PREPARING FOR YOUR TELEVISION INTERVIEW:

⭐ Wear something with lapels to make it easy to attach a clip-on mike. (Unless you enjoy strangers threading microphone wire down through your turtleneck sweater.)

⭐ Face powder reduces shine under the hot lights.

⭐ Hold yourself up; lean fifteen degrees forward.

⭐ Don't look at the camera, look at the interviewer.

AND THE MOST IMPORTANT THING:

⭐ Don't open any mystery boxes right before you're supposed to go on the air. Especially if there is a weird scratching sound coming from inside.

Act
I

I guess we'd be living in a boring, perfect world if everybody wished everybody else well.

—JENNIFER ANISTON

CHAOS.

DISASTER.

CATASTROPHE.

I've spent every one of my almost-fourteen years in Los Angeles—the world center of drama-rama. Words like *chaos, disaster,* and *catastrophe* get thrown around all the time here—even for little things like spilled coffee, freeway traffic, and two actresses wearing the same dress to the Golden Globes.

Chaos.

Disaster.

Catastrophe.

I don't throw those words around.

I earn them.

When I say chaos, I mean: a TV producer is screaming, and camera and lighting crews are fleeing my home.

When I say disaster, I mean: a set designer is in tears, and my sister's publicist is stunned silent.

When I say catastrophe, I mean: my sister is trying to jump out of her own skin.

Twenty minutes before Eva Ortiz—older sister, TV star, Young Latina of the Year—was supposed to go on the air for a live interview, she opened a mystery box.

Inside the box?

One.

Angry.

Skunk.

That's right: getting Punk'd is yesterday's celebrity nightmare; today's nightmare is getting skunk'd.

Picture it. A superhot, makeup-melting July afternoon. Max Winter, the crushworthy new MTV VJ, is here, reporting on location. He and the *TRL* crew descend on our Beverly Hills home. The crew is setting up in E's room. Max's segments are called "In the Bedroom," and usually have a chilling-in-your-crib-meets-flirting-with-cute-Max vibe.

Eva's bedroom is done in pink, black, and white. Whitest-white bedding on top of pink satin sheets, white-upholstered headboard and footboard. Round, pink shag carpet. Chrome-plated lamps. Black leather cubes that work as seats or tables. Everything is designed to accent the framed black-and-white photographs on the walls. Two rows of prints, each of Eva in different scenes from her show, *Two Sisters*.

Eva is on the bed, reviewing interview questions with her publicist, Keiko, and our mom, and sneaking glances at Max. Max is medium height, dark-skinned, with long dreads, light brown eyes, and a killer grin. He is reviewing last-minute details with his producer and cameraman. And maybe sneaking glances back at E?

Then a box arrives—special delivery by courier. Stamped with an official *Two Sisters* label, with producer Roman Capo's name on it.

Yes, there are odd scraping sounds from the box.

Yes, those might be airholes punched in the side.

Yes, E is in pre-TV prep mode, and should be left alone.

Yes, skunk spray and screaming ensue.

And sadly, yes, we have a positive ID on the accomplice: almost-fourteen-year-old female, brown hair pulled into a ponytail, brown eyes, cute enough, not counting Papa Aldo's sticker-outer ears, and wearing a crazy-guilty expression.

There's pretty much only one thing that a loving sister can think at a time like this: I *so* wish I hadn't given her that box.

FADE IN.
EXTERIOR SHOT: BEVERLY HILLS. SUMMER AFTERNOON, SUN

HIGH AND WHITE HOT OVER RED-TILED ROOF OF A LARGE SPANISH-STYLE HOME. CLOSE-UP ON: STRIPED LOUNGE CHAIRS BESIDE POOL. TWO FIGURES SIT ACROSS FROM EACH OTHER. THEY ARE SURROUNDED BY CAMERAMEN, MAKEUP ARTISTS, ETC. . . .

Max tries to save the shoot, suggesting a speedy relocation: "Maybe outside? Downwind?"

So after checking the wind direction—south, southwesterly— the lounge chairs are arranged, and the interview is set to begin.

Eva looks good. Huge hazel eyes, wide-set and uptilting. Long brown hair with reddish highlights. Wide and bright smile. Petite, Pilates-perfect body. The costume supervisor for *Two Sisters* pulled together a poolside outfit from E's closet: a hipster-prep look with tailored shorts, a white blouse, and a long string of pearls. (The pearls were borrowed from E's agent, who had been twisting them in horror.)

Eva looks good, but she smells terrible. Everyone has a skunk remedy to suggest—a tomato juice bath, dunking her in dishwashing liquid, dowsing her in perfume. Mom is driving into town to get Skunk Off. But there isn't time to try any of the remedies. It's *Total Request* Live—not *Total Request Tape-It-for-Later*.

The makeup artist darts in to dab Eva with more powder; the

10

sun is making her foundation run. Even for the few seconds she's near E, the stylist's nose is wrinkling, like it's trying to hide inside her face.

E is using every acting trick to appear calm—breathing from the diaphragm, relaxing facial muscles, visualizing a soothing space . . . but can she pull it off?

The director counts down to airtime: "Five, four, three, two . . ."

"Hello from Beverly Hills! Today, we're visiting with Eva Ortiz, sixteen-year-old breakout star of the ABC comedy hit *Two Sisters*. Hi, Eva!"

"Hi, Max!"

E and Max both have their nostrils pinched, so their voices sound a little high-pitched.

"Which video are you introducing today?" squeaks Max.

Eva tugs her ear nervously. She forces a smile. "The latest from Spilt Sugar. They're from my hometown, Anaheim, California, and they rock!" She sounds like a *Wizard of Oz* munchkin.

"Let's get to it!" Max was supposed to talk to E for another three minutes, but he throws the show back to the studio in New York. As soon as the director cues the cameras to stop filming, Max takes a big gulp of air. Then looks like he wishes he hadn't.

TRL had approached *Two Sisters* about featuring either Eva or her costar Lavender for the L.A. shoot. They went with Eva because she had more chemistry with Max. End result? An entirely new take on chemistry: they sound like they sucked down helium before going on the air.

As I watch Max wave goodbye to E (instead of the usual handshake or hug), I can read invisible words printed across his fast-retreating back: *I should have chosen Lavender. You can count on her to smell like lavender.*

I'm pretty sure I'm sporting some invisible words myself: I'm going to catch the person who skunk'd my sister, and he'd better be ready for *TRL—Total Revenge Live.*

scene 2

Sometimes it all feels like an accident.
Getting sent boxes of free designer clothing.

Standing in line at Pink's hot dog stand when Hilary Duff pulls over to say hello to E. (She watches *Two Sisters*!)

Going out for sushi at Mr. Chow's and getting seated behind the privacy screen.

Getting the cut-in-line pass at the studio theme parks. (That's extra-weird because you go through all the handicapped entrances. Celebrity-accessible seating?)

Going to a Lakers game at the Staples Center and getting courtside seats with a view of Kirsten Dunst, Salma Hayek, and Tobey Maguire—oh, yeah, and the basketball players too.

Moving from our Eva-and-Jessica-share-a-bedroom Anaheim place to a huge Spanish-style villa in Beverly Hills.

Shouldn't this life be happening to someone else?

My only plan had been to start high school this fall, struggle by in Spanish class, hang with my best friend, Leo, helping with his zine, *Avenger and Poet*. Mom working at the library, Dad at his garage. Everybody cracking up when one of Eva's TV commercials came on the screen. (*"Mom, can we talk about feminine protection?"*)

Then: TV stardom struck Eva like a lightning bolt and the whole family felt the shock. Eva's walk-on part on *Two Sisters* turned into a recurring role, then a costarring role.

The scale of all our lives changed. We're still figuring this out, but I'd guess that the good got better, and the bad got worse.

*S*peaking of worse . . .

There's probably a little something that you want to ask me. Perhaps along the lines of: "JESSICA, WHAT WERE YOU THINKING!"

Good question.

After the mystery box arrived, why did I rush it to my sister and insist that she open it? Answer: Because I believed it was from her boss, Roman. And I thought it might have been full of brownies.

Well, brownie points, anyway.

I've had some bad luck on the *Two Sisters* set in the past. Once, while I was innocently eating breakfast, guest star Ashton Kutcher's head became immersed in my marmalade. Another time, I was enjoying a ride on one of the studio golf carts when one Mr. George Clooney attacked me. ("Attack" might be a bit strong. "Playing a friendly game of pickup basketball when sideswiped in the leg due to my bad driving" is slightly more accurate.)

When it comes to Very Special Guest Stars, I've had some Very Bad Luck. So Roman has reason to dislike me, and to seriously consider banning me from the set. I thought rushing "Roman's" box to Eva, and insisting that she open it, might give him a reason to like me.

Instead: chaos, disaster, catastrophe.

Followed right now by: pain.

Pain that results from another question.

The conversation is taking place in my kitchen.

The house is cleared of crew, and the word from E's agent is that Eva and Max successfully pulled off the *TRL* interview. It wasn't great TV, but it didn't (yeah, I'm going there) stink. The world's most beautiful bulldog, my own white-and-black-and-wonderful Petunia, is chewing on my shoelaces. Our housekeeper, Mali, has whipped up my favorite snack, delicious powdery churros, which I'm tearing into bits and popping into my mouth. I have a view of our rolling backyard, with the evening sun shining off the pool. Mom, Dad, E, and I moved in just a couple of months ago, so the view is still surprising and fresh to me.

I should not be in this much pain.

But I am. Because of the question: "Do you know what's wrong with kissing?"

Please.

Please.

Please.

There are some conversations you don't want to have with your grandmother.

"Uh, Abuela . . . ?" Why did my dad have to tell her that Jeremy Jones, Eva's costar, the blond, blue-eyed Gap poster boy, is stopping by today? He and E made a plan to run lines, but my family thinks that's an excuse for him to see me. He came by last week for the first time when he lost a bet to me, and had to mow our lawn. That convinced my family that he's tired of all those six-foot-tall, skinny-as-your-pinkie model-types and interested in a petite, enjoys-a-tasty-churro girl.

"*Ay!* What's that smile for, *niña*?" Abuela has one hand clamped on her cup of coffee, one on my forearm. "You have not answered my question. Do you know what is wrong with kissing?"

I shake my head.

"Nothing!" Abuela cries. "Nothing is wrong with kissing at all. That is what is wrong with it. You see?"

Not remotely, Abuela. I nod along.

"Kissing is terrific," Abuela says emphatically. "That's why it leads to Other Things." Yes, you can actually hear the capital letters when Abuela talks.

I think of all the movies I've seen where the airplane is going down, and everyone is shouting at the pilot, "Pull up! Pull up!"

Pull up, Abuela, pull up!

"Thank you, 'buela. That's very helpful." I try to stand, but it's no go. Don't let her five-foot-nothing frame fool you—she's got a bear-trap grip.

In the reflection of the chrome refrigerator, I see my sister hiding around the corner. She's fresh from the bath, stifling her laughter and making smoochy faces at me. Very mature.

"*Ay, cariñita,* all the girls wanted my Aldo," Abuela says. I remember Papa well: short, bald, shaped like a water barrel, liked to talk about his digestion issues. "Such kisses! But do you know what happened next?"

Yes . . . this conversation got *more* uncomfortable! "Uh . . . isn't that the phone? Or the fire alarm?"

"Marriage! Dinners! Laundry! Babies! That's what!" Abuela is rolling now. "Babies—*argh!* Have you seen your father's head? Like a watermelon, that thing. And he was born with it full-sized like that. We dressed him in turtlenecks to prop it up."

Can you guess where Eva gets her love of drama from? And why Dad keeps his "watermelon" head buried under car hoods at his garage?

Abuela stops midstory. She sniffs. "What is that smell? Vinaigrette?" Superefficient Keiko downloaded a de-skunking remedy—basically a vinegar bath (one of her more unusual job responsibilities, I'm sure). Now E smells like the worst salad ever.

My sister is busted. Caught. Nabbed. She pokes her head around the corner. "Hi, Abuela."

Maybe I've inherited something from Abuela too—sleuthability.

⭐

"When I catch the person responsible, he'll pay!" Eva cries. She storms across the patio, shaking her fist at the sky. Then she pauses. "Too angry? Do you think I should go for more quietly seething?"

Jeremy looks good. Oops . . . I mean, thoughtful. Jeremy looks thoughtful. He's seated on the chair opposite me, running lines with E. "I think you're frustrated. Try it frustrated." Jeremy cues her again: "But what will you do?"

"When I catch the person responsible, he'll pay!"

Frustrated does suit the scene—and my mood.

Eva and Jeremy have been rehearsing for eleven minutes. Fully sixty seconds over the minimum time needed to sustain the I-came-over-here-to-work ruse. Unless it's not a ruse? Unless Jeremy really is visiting to improve his acting?

"Enough for today?" asks Jeremy.

Yes!

My sister could practice and prepare, run lines and rehearse all day. Her favorite thing is digging further into her character. It's only because she loves me that she says, "Yeah, that's enough. Thanks for the frustrated."

"You got it."

Ten long seconds later, my sister finally leaves.

Then it's me and Jeremy and Petunia. The last time Jeremy came over we were hanging out by the pool, and I'm almost sure that he would have kissed me except that my family could have interrupted at any minute. Abuela sharing her opinion—*Ay, Jessica! You couldn't find a Mexican boy? In Los Angeles?*—would definitely kill the joy.

Now, without talking about it, we head out to the lawn, finding a spot where a flowering pear tree partially shields my house from view. Jeremy is rolling a ball around, and Petunia is trying to paw it.

Jeremy looks so sweet playing with my dog that I lean right over and kiss him.

In.

My.

Head.

In my real life, I pull up some clumps of grass and sprinkle them over Petunia. Some girls might launch their lips at the boy they like, but I'm not like that. Confession: I'm a recovering shy girl.

Mostly under control, but sometimes a wave of nervousness can still find me. My head dips to the ground, and my brain freezes. All my shyness-control tips get mixed up: *Don't Breathe! Panic Deeply!*

Jeremy asks, "So what happened today?"

Everything happened today!

I explain about how the mystery box arrived—how it seemed to be from *Two Sisters*, how I encouraged Eva to open it, and the trouble that followed. Then I tell him the saddest part: "And in the middle of the interview with Max, Eva made her Just Go signal."

"What?"

"You know, a getaway signal? If E thinks that a fan is too aggressive or a crowd is about to get pushy, she touches her ear, and everyone in my family knows to get her out. She didn't even realize it, but she made that exact signal on the air."

Jeremy nods. "Cool."

"Huh?"

"That your family looks out for Eva." Jeremy makes me wonder what his family is like. "My mom would need some serious retail therapy after a morning like that."

"Lots of little blue boxes, huh?"

Jeremy gives me a sidelong glance. "You're a Tiffany's girl?"

Yikes. I might have accidentally Googled an interview—or two or ten—with his mom, and found out about her love of jewelry, modern art, and couture fashion.

OMG—what else do I know about Jeremy that I'm not supposed to know?

I blush. "Not really."

THINGS JEREMY AND I TALK ABOUT
WHILE WE TEASE PETUNIA WITH HER PINK
RUBBER TRIANGLE:

⭐ Pets: (He'd love to have a dog; I do *not* admit how I whined "but it's so hard to fit into our new Hollywood life" to soften Mom up for Petunia.)

⭐ Vacation spots: There is a rumor that *Two Sisters* will be shooting on location. Jeremy's first choice: Kenya; mine: Costa Rica.

⭐ School: Jeremy has only ever been to set-school (a few hours a day with a tutor at the studio); I'm off to a new school this fall. I've been wearing my red

Academy jacket to get used to the idea.

⭐ **What's good: (iTunes; Krispy Kremes; Starbucks caramel-apple cider; all dogs, even the little ratty ones; and snowboarding—yeah, I'm so faking it about that one!)**

⭐ **Project Stop Skunk: He's going to help me get the baddie behind it.**

Then my cell starts to sing. Classic Gwen Stefani: "Long Way to Go."

I check the caller. My own mom. Calling from my own house. On the other side of this tree. It's unlikely that I will ever be cool as long as my mom loves me.

"Yes, Mom, I'll be up in a minute. . . . Okay . . . Chinese food on the table." I click off, shrugging at Jeremy. "Dinnertime." Then I look at my watch. "Wow! It's later than I thought."

"No problem. Cool song on your phone."

"I could put it on your phone." As soon as the words are out, they sound brassy. If Jeremy was just a friend, it'd be nothing. But for whatever we are, programming his phone sounds pushy.

Then he says, "Really? Thanks!"

And it's all cool.

In fact, I don't think the moment can get much better.

Until suddenly it does.

Get much better.

"We should have a signal," Jeremy suggests.

"A Just Go signal?"

"Not exactly." Jeremy touches his ear.

Then he leans over and kisses me. A slow press of lips that leaves me a second to wonder why a kiss should send a zing-zing through every piece of me. Then I'm not wondering.

I just am.

Happy, that is.

Zing-zing happy.

Mom must hate the happy. All too soon we're interrupted by another call from the house.

How does she know?

When I finally say goodbye to Jeremy, and make it to dinner, nothing can bother me. Not Eva's soapy-over-stinky smell. Not Mom promising to give me a long talk "about boys." Not Abuela promising me a longer talk "about boys." Not Dad glowering at his dumplings every time the word "boy" comes up. Not even a fortune cookie that tells me: *Brightest happiness is briefest*.

Eva gets a cookie that says: *Weeds of betrayal flourish in your garden*.

Lucky Chang's House of Happy Joy should consider a new name. Or a new fortune-teller.

scene 3

Two Sisters sends a car to pick up my sister every morning. Mom joins Eva on the set to deal with contract or publicity issues; I join her on the set to watch her back. (And sometimes her costar.)

I'm dressed in comfortable clothes—red Keds, white shorts, checkered sleeveless top under my red Academy jacket, with my bag thrown over my shoulder. I don't know where Project Stop Skunk will take me today.

Keiko is already in the car when it pulls up. She brings a breakfast offering from the Bagel Broker for the crew. Eva doesn't hang out with the lighting and camera workers, but she knows how much they have to do with how she looks on your television screen. And she knows how happy a fresh batch of danishes makes them.

Keiko's choppy-cut, bright platinum hair swings around her dark eyes as she exclaims, "Eva, you were amazing on *TRL*! You and Max had awesome chemistry!"

Eva looks doubtful. "You think so, Key?"

"I don't think it! I know it!"

Mom sighs. "It's a good thing it was a live shoot, not pre-recorded."

Huh? "If it had been taped, we could have stopped for a while, and started up when . . . everything was back to normal."

"Not exactly." Keiko looks at me like I ate a big bowl of wishful thinking for breakfast. "People *think* they have more control with a taped show. They assume the film editor is on their side, but the editor is on the side of the best show. If today's show had been taped, they would have let Eva freshen up and redo the scene. But then they would have cut that interview with shots of the skunk disaster, and spliced it all with some music like . . . what's that song you like? 'Smells Like Funk'?"

All's fair in love and war—and television?

"But the way it turned out, Eva, you rocked!" Part of Keiko's job is selling stories—or versions of stories—about Eva to the press. Sometimes she has to sell the stories to E as well. We get stuck in traffic on the 101, and by the time we pull through the studio's gates, Keiko practically has Eva believing that Max's "In the Bedroom" segment should be changed to "Outside and Downwind" from now on. She's that good.

Today we're going to the Warner Brothers lot for filming. *Two Sisters* is renting a water tank for a rescue scene. Whenever filmmakers need tons of water in a controlled space—think *Titanic*—they use the tanks.

The *Sisters* writers are getting especially creative because the competition this year has got real bite. (That *Snake Bait* reality series is coming on strong. Even I want to know what happens to poor little Timmy.)

In the ongoing story line, the "two sisters," Lavender and Paige, and their pretty Latina neighbor, Eva, and the brooding-but-cute boy next door, Jeremy, are regular Boston high school students by day, but work together to foil a petnapping ring after school. Today's rescue attempt involves a water tank, with Eva playing the hero, Lavender playing the helpless screamer, and Mr. Whiskers the Third playing his fine feline self. Jeremy and Paige arrive at the end of the drama with nothing to do but look good in their bathing suits.

The car drops us off by the *Two Sisters* trailers. Mom and Keiko head off to talk with the costume supervisor about Eva's wardrobe. Mom was raging about the bikini they had suggested—"string with a gland condition!" (Eva will be in a full wet suit under a raincoat, with earmuffs, before Mom is done.)

E gets launched headfirst into the world of acting.

As in Lavender and Paige *acting* sorry about E's MTV (Maximum Trauma Viewed) experience.

"Oh, sugar, you pulled it off! You did." Lavender would never admit how furious she was that MTV chose Eva over her—but her satisfied smirk says it all. She is dressed in a floating indigo top over tight purple jeans. Her earrings, sandals, handbag, and hair clips are all in various shades of (*wait for it* . . .) lavender. She swings her long dark hair and widens her violet eyes. Her acting coach probably told her big eyes plus Southern accent equals sincerity.

With Paige's green eyes, killer cheekbones, and general golden-blondness, the former model is rocking the California-beach-babe look in expensively torn-up jeans and a tank top. "Good thing it's television, not smellevision!" she says with a laugh. "I'm kidding! You so could not tell if you didn't know." Short pause. "But everyone knows."

"Ah guess you saw Hollywood Hype this morning?" Lavender says.

"No, I didn't." Eva's smile is locked in place. She didn't so much miss the gossip column as tear the Life and Style section to bits before anyone could read it.

Lavender recites:

Smells Like Trouble

MTV hottie Max Winter and Latina lovely Eva Ortiz made pee-you-tiful music together when their interview was stink-bombed by a skunk. How did the stinker sneak onto the Ortiz property? Who nose?

"Thanks, Lavender." Eva ups the wattage on her smile to force-field level. Sometimes a competitor with a gift for perfectly memorizing lines is not easy to take. And did Hollywood Hype really write in that happy cackle at the end of the piece?

"Pee-you?" says Paige, slowly. "Oh, I get it!"

A costar on a five-second time delay presents challenges too.

Lavender rolls her eyes my way. "You must be Eva's baby sister," she drawls. "You do look something like her, shug." Lavender refuses to remember me. And I refuse to admit it bothers me. Like a fly's feet, her attention never lands on me for long. Now she turns toward the sound of an approaching vehicle. "Is that the writers? Ah have a few suggestions on the scene."

Lavender has been fighting the Eva-saves-the-day slant since the first script read-through. And she's not shy about pitching suggestions to the writers. Something about her Georgia-sweetness means she gets thought of as "charmingly persistent" instead of "screamingly annoying."

But it's not the writers in a studio van, it's a huge chrome-and-leather Harley-Davidson. The roar pounds my eardrums. I'm not a mechanic's daughter for nothing—I see where the regular exhaust system was switched out for straight exhaust pipes—the kind that increase the motor's noise.

The rider is wearing a trucker hat, not a helmet, so I get a good look as he circles. Stubble-faced and dark-eyed with short black hair. Small silver hoops stuck through his eyebrow. Tight blue T-shirt, jeans, beat-up boots. A tattoo of barbed wire trails up his forearm.

"Lavender, is that your new boyfriend?" Paige shouts over the engine's howl.

It's hard to stay up-to-date with Lavender's love life, so I've prepared this circle-the-current-answers format for easy reference.

Lavender's new boyfriend is
a singer in a boy band
a reality TV "star"
an oil-money heir

She and her boyfriend are
making out
dirty dancing
talking about hair products

When Lavender gets into
a huge slap-fight with
A costar
A reporter
A peace activist

Lavender blames the
trouble on her agent,
and immediately
fires him
sues him

reorganizes the feng shui
in his office so that all
the furniture is facing evil

*(Hint: There's not neces-
sarily only one correct answer.)*

"Yes, that's Murphy."

Paige pouts. "I can't believe you're dating someone from a rival network!"

"Both shows are by Banks Brothers Studios, and besides, shug, reality TV is totally different from what we do."

I'm picturing one of those poor *Snake Bait* contestants when Paige says, "What's his show called? *Cranky Pants*?"

"*Crank Pranksters*." Now I remember—a reality show that challenges teams to outprank each other, and Murphy is the host. Hot sauce on the toothbrush, putting salt in the sugar shaker, covering toilet seats with plastic wrap . . . it all seems to crack guys up, but most girls don't get it at all.

Sometimes I'm especially proud to be a girl.

"Anyway, he's just doing that till his band, Runny Snots, takes off." Translation: He's doing that forever. If the lyrics are as bad as the band name, those songs will never sell.

I kind of remember some tabloids saying that Murphy was the new hotness, but then all the talk about him died out.

I steal a peek at Eva, and I see that she's here . . . but not here. In her mind, she's running through the Mr. Whiskers rescue. *Practice, practice, practice.*

Murphy turns off the Harley and calls to Lavender. Out of his mouth comes . . . pure New York. Make that pure NEW YAWK. "Yo, Lavvy!" His voice is set for drowning out taxis and ambulance sirens.

Lavender smiles—though the nickname "Lavvy," sounding so close to "lavatory," would typically result in a death-by-purple-pumps-pounding. Murphy and Lavvy go together like polka dots and prints—nothing matches. "C'mere, check out the new ride!"

"Text me when it's time to head over to the water tank," Lavender tells Paige.

Jealous costar, snubbed by *TRL*, has boyfriend who specializes in pranks? I'm not exactly going to need my advanced degree in *CSI* watching to get to the bottom of Project Stop Skunk.

Am I?

*F*ade to black.

In a script, those words appear at the end of a scene. Never at the beginning.

But what we're looking at here is a scene that faded to black before it began.

The tank is tall, clear, and round. It's supposed to look like a giant glass of water. The cameras are positioned outside the tank to get shots of the actors underwater.

Water has to be water-colored for that to work.

A tank of dark ink? Not camera-friendly.

Somebody sabotaged the set. The water has been dyed black. No one knows if it would be safe for the actors to go in it. The tank isn't permanently damaged, but by the time the water is drained and the tank refilled, the *Sisters* window for shooting will be over. The new *Aquagirl* movie has every tank in town booked solid for twelve weeks starting tomorrow.

Roman is wearing a look best described as "pre-seizure." I'd like to grab a minute with producer-man to confirm that he didn't send my sister a skunk, or lend a mailing label to a skunk, but—

a new vein bulges along his forehead—now doesn't seem like the full-on ideal time.

The Warner Brothers representative tries to calm Roman down. She uses her most soothing, please-don't-give-yourself-a-heart-attack-on-my-lot voice. "Perhaps it was an accident? Or you asked for something that was misinterpreted—"

Roman cuts her off. "Get me Security . . . no, forget those rent-a-cops, get me the real thing! I want the LAPD on this, *now*." A blue pulse beats at the edge of Roman's eye. Seeing me usually makes the pulse beat more angrily, so I duck behind Lighting Guy Bob. Eva's generous danish donation gives me plenty to hide behind.

The WB rep is pounding numbers on her cell phone when Lavender glides up to her. She takes the rep and Roman aside. Whatever she tells Roman, he does not want to hear. Roman throws an angry glance at where Murphy had been standing, but the guy has melted away.

I can't hear what Lavender is saying, but a few seconds later, Roman throws up his hands. "Okay! Okay! Lavender, you win. No cops. Can we figure out some way to save this shoot? Al? Where's Al?"

Al Maggio is the *Two Sisters* head writer. Al is green-cheese-colored, with small gray eyes lost behind round glasses, wrapped in wrinkles from his forehead to his baggy pants. Looking at him reminds me that I should probably turn the kitchen plants toward the sun when we get back home.

For obvious reasons, everyone calls him Anxious Al. Is he anxious because he has to come up with scripts every week about teen girls, and he never was one, or even talked to one as a teen? Or is the anxiety a result of his personal experiment to see how much ultra-caffeinated Red Bull one human body can withstand? Either way, the guy is jumpier than a bag of kangaroos. And that was before the big tank rescue turned into the big blackout. The rumor is that the camera operators have a bet going to see if Al will crack up before he gets fired, or get fired before he cracks up.

Al jitters up to Roman. Usually, Roman, Al, and the junior writers spend countless hours perfecting scenes and dialogue. Can Al write us out of this mess?

"Friends, Roman, countrymen . . . ," begins Al. Then his eyes start twitching, settling at last for a loopy stare into space. There is a long, terrible moment when everyone waits for Al to say something more. I can almost hear the blood pounding in Roman's head.

Into the awful silence, one of the junior writers speaks. "Roman?"

"Yes, Carlton?"

"I have an idea—just putting an oar in, if it helps." Carlton is young, with slicked-back white-blond hair and black square-framed glasses. Most people in L.A. dress casually, but he's rocking a preppy East Coast vibe in a pink Lacoste polo and khakis.

Carlton throws out his suggestion, and Roman actually starts to look calmer. He never looks peaceful—the stress level that most people need an SAT exam to work up to is pretty much normal for him.

Roman looks at Carlton. "That's not terrible, babe."

The new plan: changing the water rescue to a tree rescue. Also on the Warner lot is the "Park Boulevard" set, a block of Boston-style row houses looking onto a park and fountain (the fountain is the one used in the opening of *Friends*.) It fits with the Boston setting of *Two Sisters*, allows for a rescue, and takes advantage of being on location.

"How fast can you write it, Quick Carl?" asks Roman.

"Quick." Carlton smiles at the new nickname.

"I'll help," says Amber. Tiny, chain-smoking, sharp-eyed, she's another junior writer. The rumor is that she is being groomed to replace Al. "Anxious Amber" has a ring to it.

There are a few unhappy faces.

Tommy "Pet-Man" Peterson, Mr. Whiskers the Third's trainer, is upset that the work he did preparing for the water rescue won't be used. "I've been digging fur balls out of my bathtub for weeks!"

Eva and Lavender wear the same blank, closed look on their faces: they got cut.

For the revised scene, Jeremy and Paige will be the rescuers. Carlton didn't say it out loud, but everyone knows that they are the two actors who can best get by with no rehearsal.

Jeremy has spent his entire life in the business—from diapers to driving permit. If you asked him to unicycle around the lot twirling flaming bowling pins, he'd say something like: "Oh, you mean like I did on *Carnival of Stars* when I was eight?" Paige has been acting for only a couple of years—she started as a model— but she's an instinctual performer. She has a sixth sense about how her character would respond. Lavender and Eva could take on a wider variety of roles, but for the parts that Paige can play, she does better with less rehearsing.

Mom isn't happy with the change. Not that she cares about screen time, but because Eva is unhappy. Mom tries to joke: "I bet you think I dyed the water to keep you out of that bikini!" Eva tries to laugh.

We can't even go home because Eva has one line at the end of the scene: "You did it!" As in, *I* didn't get a chance to.

Roman squeezes permission out of the Warner Brothers group to shoot at the Park Boulevard set, and the technical crew is frantically setting up. "The light keeps changing," grumbles Lighting Guy Bob.

Well, yes, Bob. We're outdoors. That light is called the sun and it changes all day. Not much we can do about that. The property master comes up with a ladder, the costume supervisor swaps in new clothes, the writers polish the dialogue, the actors get into character, and the cameras get into position.

I'm standing next to the writers to get a good view of Jeremy at work. Jeremy looks over and gives me his half smile. I feel the grin on my face getting big and goofy so I put my hand over my mouth.

Beside me, Amber beckons Roman over, waving her cell phone. It must be an important call because she's risking Roman's ray-of-death glare. "It's a lead on the ink incident."

Roman hurries over and grabs the phone. His eyes darken, and someone is in serious trouble. All I know for sure is that whoever Mr. Stressed-Out Producer is angry with this time, it can't be me. I had nothing to do with the inking.

Roman turns. His eyes drill into me.

He whispers two cold words right in my ear: *"It's you."*

*I*f I was the sister of a stylist, camera operator, writer, director, or producer, Roman would have bounced me and my bad luck long ago. If I was Roman's own sister—his mother! his *abuela*!—he would have bounced me. But I'm Eva's sister, and Eva is a star.

Stars are hard to mess with.

FOR THREE REASONS:

⭐ **Audiences notice if stars are replaced. (When a TV actress gets pregnant, they give her big pillows or giant handbags to hide behind—they don't drop in a whole new person.)**

⭐ **No one knows what makes a star "connect." Think about your favorite star—**

Orlando? Jennifer? Jake? Beyoncé? All gorgeous, of course, but what they have that makes them stars isn't something that can be broken down into a recipe. Three cups good-looking meets two tablespoons talented plus a pinch of sweet doesn't sum it up. What they have is . . . a connection with you and me. All of Hollywood wants to know *why* we feel it, and who we're going to feel it about next, but they can't quite crack the code.

No one knows what makes a star *stop* connecting. Is her new role too harsh, too far from the expected? Or is there some matter in her personal life—say, a sibling being banned from the set—that dims the connection? Who knows? So don't mess with the mojo.

"Anything you'd like to tell me, babe?" Roman stiff-arms me over to the far side of the makeup trailer. He slants his dark eyes (and brings his bad breath) closer to my face.

Try: *Get your hands off me, psycho stress case!* Which sadly comes out as: "No, sir. Nothing, sir."

"Are you sure? It will go a lot easier for you if you confess." What? It's hard to believe Roman helps write the show when he comes out with dialogue like that.

I should probably play dumb-girly. I'll get away quicker, but I won't get what I want. I want answers. "Confess? What do you mean? Have *the police* found something?"

Roman's face flames. Whatever Lavender told him means he can't call the cops. What *did* she tell him? Something about Murphy? The inking? The skunking?

He tightens his grip on my elbow. "Warner Brothers has a witness who spotted someone with a red jacket and brown ponytail dumping the dye into the tank."

I look down. My Academy jacket has never looked . . . redder. Even my hair—tied off my face with a red band—is incriminating me. Suddenly, I know how the burger patties feel right before Dad fires up the grill.

Amber appears around the corner, shouting, "Roman! Mom alert! Now!"

Roman releases me. *That's right, mister. Nobody messes with Mama Ortiz's little girl!*

But Amber is pointing through the window of the makeup trailer to the small TV set up inside. And the mom she's pointing to?

I'd almost rather be related to Roman.

Almost.

*P*aige has the sad celebrity fate to have a mom who wishes that she was the star instead of her daughter. Sometimes mom and daughter are battling each other in court over Paige's being an emancipated teenager (meaning: she divorced her mom), or else they're hanging at clubs, sharing cigarettes and size-skinny jeans.

When Roman realizes that Mama Paige is about to be interviewed on live television, he drops my elbow and turns to Amber. "Where is she?"

"Paige locked herself in the camera van. Her scene is done, but she's got that charity fashion show tonight." Paige is transitioning away from modeling, but she still walks the runway if it's for a good cause. "Jeremy is trying to talk to her."

Roman forgets about me, and takes off to find Paige.

Amber charges into the makeup trailer, where the stylists are gathered around the TV. I follow Amber, peeking around her back.

On-screen, the reporter, his hair and smile equally stiff, leans toward his guest. The camera pans to a long, knife-thin woman stabbed into a soft chair. Her face is hard-boned and thickly smeared with makeup. Under the orangey tan, fake blond hair, and football player eyeliner, I can see that she must have looked a lot like Paige once. Spooky.

"*Inside Hollywood* welcomes Paige Carey's mom, Linda."

"Thrilled to be here, Ben!"

"I have a question for you, Linda, but it's a bit difficult to phrase. . . ."

"Don't be shy! I get it all the time. All the time. How could I *possibly* be old enough to have a teenage daughter?" Linda beams. "Starting young! That's my secret." She turns away from Ben to face the camera directly—a blatant violation of one of my top five TV-interview tips. "But, girls, that's not my recommendation. Teen mom-hood is tough mom-hood."

Beside me, Amber mutters, "She was *twenty-eight* when she had Paige."

"Actually, my question was, why have you chosen to speak out publicly about your daughter's problems?"

Mama Paige blinks. Her eyes shine green, round as a doll's. "To show my support. Since Paige threw me out of her life . . . again . . .

this is the only way left for me to communicate with her. Call Mama, baby!" She dabs at her dry eyes. "I'm an actress myself—drama, comedy, dramedy—so I understand her pain."

If she thinks she's selling out her daughter for a few seconds of fame, it doesn't show on her face. But that might be the Botox.

"What do you mean?"

"I couldn't see Paige on her birthday last week! But I have my sources. I know her day was ruined by that creepy secret admirer!"

Paige had thought Jeremy was her secret admirer, but it turned out to be an assistant to Lighting Guy Bob. The admirer was fully less than admirable—selling stories to the gossip columns to get money to pursue Paige. With help from me, Jeremy, my dad, and even Paige, he was caught.

"Secret admirer?" Ben looks interested. "What can you tell us about him?"

"I can tell you he's a *beeeep beep*! *Beepity beep,* and *beep,* and *beep*." All that squeaks by the censor are punctuation and conjunctions.

"Linda, this is a family show."

"Oh *beep*. I mean, sorry."

"Thank you for your time."

44

The camera is on the interviewer as the credits roll, but I can hear Mama Paige say, "Can you mention that I'm a former Miss Whispering Pines?"

The TV clicks off.

Okay. I think I have to go hug my mom now.

Amber and the stylists are expressing how bad they feel for Paige by rehashing everything her mom said. Steve, the head hairstylist, tosses orange blush on his face to get the full effect. "And she was wearing an exact copy of Paige's dress from the 'Hamster's Wheel of Misfortune' episode!" he cackles.

I slip out of the trailer and land right in the middle of a big fight. And it's all about Project Stop Skunk.

scene 5

"Murphy, Ah told you this has gone too far!"

I pull back behind the trailer before Lavender can spot me. She is giving her boyfriend a serious telling-off.

"Keep your voice down, Lavvy!" Murphy may think he's being quiet, but he's the kind of New Yorker who doesn't come with an inside voice.

"Ah will not! Four minutes to twenty seconds! Mah role got cut from four minutes to under half a minute. Less airtime is the opposite of what Ah want! Did your brain have a blackout as well as that—"

Murphy interrupts. "Lav, you haveta believe me, I'd never . . . waitaminute." His voice drops. "Who wears red sneakers around here?"

I look at my feet. Guilty.

I realize that the toes of my sneakers are pointing out around the corner.

Shuffle. Shuffle. I creep farther back, but it's no use. Lavender and Murphy have disappeared. She had been accusing him of inking the pool. Hadn't she?

Grr . . . I blew a major lead.

I'm leaning against the trailer, piecing together everything Murphy said, when I hear a voice calling my name.

"Jessica!"

"Hi, Keiko."

"Your mom is looking for you, babe. We're ready to go."

"Okay." Keiko dials down the enthusiasm when she talks to me versus Eva. But she always tells it to me the way she sees it. I ask her, "Do Murphy and Lavender seem like a strange couple to you?"

"Loudmouth bad boy meets Southern belle?" Keiko shrugs. "It's a total *faux*mance."

"A what?"

"Fauxmance. You know? A romance to help your career. Lavender is up for the part of Naughty in the new *Tough Girls* movie. Getting seen with Murphy is a fast way to shake up her image."

"Fake-kissing someone for work. . . ."

"Pretty much what she does for a living. She also fake-hugs, fake-kicks, and fake-likes."

Weird. But I guess even at school there seemed to be couples who were together for the show of being together. And they weren't getting paid for it.

"Supposedly Lavender's mom doesn't like Murphy, and that's why she's not hanging around the set as usual, but *I* think that's just to keep Lavvy from looking like such a mama's girl."

"C'mon, Keiko, everyone argues with their mom about guys. Not everything is about publicity."

Keiko raises an eyebrow but makes no reply as we head over to the Town Car. I take one last look around for Jeremy; no luck. The windows on the car are rolled down, so I can see that my sister has an unexpected expression on her face: happy. Not what I would have predicted after watching her part get cut.

Keiko and I join my sister in the backseat. Mom sits up front with the driver.

"What's up, E?"

"We're going to Mexico!"

"*Bueno!* How long is the drive?"

"We're not *driving*." E's tone implies that I'd suggested she walk to a foreign country in her precious Jimmy Choo sling-backs. *Excuse me, Princess Hollywood.* "The show is going to be shooting there! We fly down on Thursday!"

The writers had wanted to film at a foreign location all last season, but the show's backer, Ivan Banks of Banks Brothers Studios, was holding out.

"Mr. Moneybags gave the green light?"

"*Sí!*" says Eva. "I guess he realized the great storytelling potential of a Mexican setting."

As usual, Keiko has the story-behind-the-story. "Plus he just bought the biggest hotel in Cancún, and the shoot will create millions of dollars of instant publicity and tourist business."

Mom nods. "They must've been planning the trip for weeks but couldn't announce it till the hotel sale was public."

I lean over the seat to talk to my mom. "Eva is going, so I have to go too!"

She sighs. "Where, exactly, is the 'have to' in this scenario?"

The fastest route to a yes from Mom involves academics. Wish me luck. "You know that I'm taking Spanish this year, right?"

Mom nods. Slowly. And of course she knows that I'm trading in my Anaheim school for a pricey Beverly Hills Catholic academy.

"The Academy class is going to be so far ahead of my old school. I have some serious catching up to do. Total language immersion is key. Plus, I'll get more in touch with my Mexican roots."

"And this has nothing to do with Jeremy Jones?"

"Who?"

Mom squints at me.

I may have overplayed that.

Eva comes to the rescue. "Mom, Keiko told me that the show is putting me up in a two-thousand-dollar-a-night suite."

"What! That's an outrageous expense!" My mom's thoughts have immediately gone to all the more humane uses for a couple thousand bucks. She's bighearted that way. "Why, you, Lavender, and Paige should be sharing a room anyway. Like a big slumber party." She's bighearted, but deluded. My sister's costars wouldn't share oxygen with Eva if they could help it.

"Not gonna happen, Mom."

Mom is about to head down the road to social justice and role models when Eva ably diverts her. "If Jessica could come with me, it would be like the suite was a thousand dollars a night for each of us."

"What a bargain," Mom says darkly.

"Plus, Jess could be my chaperone in the wilds of Mexico."

Mom agrees. "All right, Jessica, you're going." Before I can cheer, she adds, "You, Eva, and me."

There's little chance of Mom not coming, but it's worth a try. "What about your big book club reunion Thursday? The study of the role of financial freedom in *Little Women* sounded so . . . fascinating."

Eva shoots me a look. I've overplayed my hand again.

But at least I'm going to Mexico! *Olé!*

*E*ver-capable Keiko keeps one eye out the window during our drive home. She and Mom exchange a look. "Still with us, Mrs. Ortiz."

Mom nods.

I look out the window and see that we're being followed by a 4x4 with tinted windows.

The driver of the 4x4 goes by a lot of names. Mom would call him a "telephoto-wielding bottom-feeder." Keiko would call him "part of the game." The tabloids would call him a "paparazzo."

The 4x4 stays on our tail. For a moment, I think he's going to peel off when we pass a former sitcom star in a car in the next lane—I can't remember his name; one of the cute guy's dorky best friends. He is hanging out the window to make sure everyone can see him. But the paparazzo doesn't take the bait. Available equals boring.

Mom makes the decision. "I don't want him to follow us home. Let's give him the shot." She turns to the driver. "Pull into the nearest convenience center, please."

"Yes, ma'am."

"Telephoto-wielding bottom-feeder," Mom mutters. Do I know her or what?

Keiko preps my sister. "When you go into the store, be friendly, buy one jug of milk, and leave."

"Milk?"

"Sure. We might as well take the opportunity to try to get a 'Got Milk?' spot. Make sure they don't bag the milk."

Eva sighs. "This is *so* Stars—They're Just Like Us!" (The dreaded section in the tabloids where celebs get caught taking out their garbage, or just looking like garbage.)

"There are worse ways to be 'Like Us' than buying milk," Keiko warns. "And I don't care where you have an itch. Don't scratch! Don't pick, don't pull, don't pinch!"

The car stops at a 7-Eleven. Eva gets out.

The 4x4 pulls into the lot, grabbing a spot with a view of the entrance to the store. Eva goes inside.

Mom gets a call on her cell while we wait for E to come back. Keiko turns to me: "You never know where these guys are. Remember when Paige got papped smoking outside that lung cancer benefit? *Ugh.*"

I guess there's one good thing about the skunking: it wasn't caught on camera.

My sister steps out of the store, milk carton visible in hand. The pap gets his photo and pulls away.

"Got milk," E says, getting into the car. "Let's go."

Keiko nods. "Good. Nothing scandalicious."

"Keiko, please, that's not a word." Mom's librarian instincts flare at strange moments.

"No, Mrs. Ortiz, it's a way of life."

Mom frowns. "Eva, I just got a call from your agent. You're going to have to face the bottom-feeders one more time tonight."

Act
II

Acting really is like a big poker game, isn't it?
When do you show your cards? Because we don't want to
know everything up front, do we?

—CHARLIZE THERON

I f my sister is riding to the rescue, she's going to arrive looking fabulous.

Paige's agent asked the cast to appear at Paige's fashion show tonight. The idea (which the other agents love) is to create a story about "the super-supportive *Two Sisters* family" to leak steam from the "Paige's crazy mom outs freaky stalker" story. Usually "supportive" has a hard time winning newspaper space over "crazy-freaky," but the *Two Sisters* cast will be dressed up and smiling for the cameras. "Fantastic-looking" has a fighting chance versus "crazy-freaky."

The show's costume supervisor, Hélène, brought the dresses over. Eva is in a belted black Gucci sheath dress with borrowed diamond-drop earrings by Harry Winston. She did her own hair, a tight French braid.

My dress is a whirl of orange-blue-yellow, cut to the knee, with medium shoulder straps. I blew out my hair, which E took one look at and redid, clipping it into a soft halo around my face. Hélène Marcy didn't have to bring over a dress for me, but she's one of my friends on the set. I'm always asking her for inside fashion scoop. "Any fashion tips, Hélène?"

"Red is the new red." Now you know.

The limo arrives to pick up Mom, E, and me. Around-the-clock Keiko is already sitting in the back.

"Key, do you live in this limo?"

"If you need me to, Eva!" Keiko is dressed in a black pantsuit. Usually Keiko is quite fashionable, but for public events she dresses to underscore that she's "support staff."

The fashion show is being held at the Tropicana Bar, the Asian-inspired outdoor club at Hollywood's Roosevelt Hotel. The candlelit pool will be covered with a runway, and the models will parade under the palm trees. It's a benefit for the Sunshine Children's Charities, with dresses to be auctioned at the end of the night.

Keiko gives us the scoop on how the evening might play out. The entrance will be mobbed with photographers and fashion groupies. The groupies will be dressed to impress—the tradition is to pass an unneeded ticket to the best-dressed fan.

If we see Paige on the red carpet or in the lobby, Eva will go over to her for some kissy-face photos. If she doesn't see Paige then, E will save the love for an aftershow photo session. Keiko isn't sure how the show will open. Some designers open with a short film—

like Kenneth Cole's social message minimovies ("What You Stand For Is More Important Than What You Stand In"). Some houses, like Imitation of Christ, go with live performances.

"Have you ever seen Paige in a show?" Eva asks Keiko.

"No, but I've heard she's a natural. Most models, except the Brazilians, have to take walking lessons, but not Paige."

"'Walking lessons'?" Mom says skeptically. "Now we're telling young women that they don't know how to walk?" Mom is freaked enough that acting places huge pressure on Eva to be skinny, smiley, perky, and perfect—but at least E can hide out behind a character. With modeling, you're judged by your face, your body, and your walk.

"There are different walks," Keiko explains. A 'Versace walk' means shake-it-like-you-might-break-it. 'Street' means looking straight ahead, no swish. 'Summer' means a slower walk, with a hip sway."

The limo rolls down Hollywood Boulevard, its Walk of Fame sidewalks set with pink and bronze stars. We pull to a stop directly across from Mann's Chinese Theatre, home of the handprints of the stars. The words HOTEL ROOSEVELT glow in neon over a large white hotel. The red carpet stretches from the curb to the door.

We wait in the limo for the celebs who arrived before us to exit their car.

"Look, the show is live," says Keiko. She has flipped to *Inside Hollywood* on the limo's mini-TV.

Pressed against the limo's windows, I watch Paige step out of a silver convertible.

That's funny, that looks like Jeremy's car.

Then I see who Paige is with.

And I don't feel like laughing.

scene 2

In *Us Weekly*, Paige usually winds up under the heading "When Bad Clothes Happen to Good People." The hot trends are baby doll dresses and cowboy style. Most fashionistas choose one of the looks at a time, but tonight Paige is wearing a sky blue chiffon dress covered in tiny bows paired with a brown cowboy hat and boots. The cowboy hat is decorated with suns, I guess for the Sunshine Children's Charities.

How pretty is Paige? Pictures of her in that ensemble will sell blue dresses—*and* sunshiny cowboy hats. But maybe she looks so good because of the decoration on her arm—Jeremy Jones.

Jeremy is wearing a midnight blue blazer, a matching untucked shirt, tuxedo pants, and . . . a huge smile.

The reporters converge on Paige. Her grin falters, and Jeremy puts his hand on her back. At the same moment, Mom takes my hand. Mom, Eva, and I are all looking out the side window together, listening to the interview on the TV.

"Paige!" says a reporter. "Your costars are coming out to support you. Does that help you deal with the rumors started by your mom?"

Paige blinks her big green eyes. "I work with a wonderful cast. We're like a rainstorm; no single drop of water can fall on its own."

"So true, Paige!" The reporter plunges on. "So, Ms. Carey, you and Mr. Jones certainly look cozy tonight. Has your working relationship become something . . . more?"

Ugh. Is it me or do reporters only care about *one thing*?

Paige smiles. "Why say when you can show?"

What did she mean by . . . ?

NO.

NO.

NO.

The moment unrolls in hideous slow motion. Paige grabs Jeremy by the back of the neck. She pulls his head toward her, and plants this huge kiss right on his lips.

The word that best describes the kiss (after *sickening*) is *thorough*.

I wait for him to push her off . . .

and wait . . .

and wait.

Instead, he kisses her back! He puts his hands in her hair and then dips her low in his arms, kissing her every second. The photographers' flashes reflect off their blond heads.

The reporter laughs. "Young love! Signing off, for *Inside Hollywood*, this is Betze Urbane."

I feel sick. Some fist has reached out, grabbed my guts, and won't let go.

Mom pulls me against her. "Oh, *m'ija*," she says, hugging tight. "I'm sorry. You liked him, didn't you?"

As if *that's* what I want to be reminded of.

Mom is sad. Eva is furious. "That creep! That no-talent toad! I'm going to step on his lines, blow his cues, and steal his scenes! Don't worry, Jess. He's not getting away with this." My sister's fists are clenched, and her eyes are crackling. "And neither is that *blank* Paige. We're out of here."

Keiko quickly passes our tickets out the window to a few of the fashion groupies. The limo pulls back into traffic.

"Paige Carey?" Keiko mutters. "Her teeth are brighter than she is."

Me? I'm quiet. I'm numb.

Time doesn't pass quite right when you're numb, so I don't know how long it takes us to get back to Beverly Hills.

Somehow I'm in my room, stretched across my bed. I'm in my slip. My dress is hanging over the door, empty as a dream.

I rub Petunia's warm belly while she pants in my face. Unconditional doggie love—the only way to go. Life lesson learned.

At my side, my sister is finger-combing my hair. "Jess, talk to me. How do you feel?"

Those might sound like the words of a loving sister—and they are. But they are also the words of an actress. Eva's always got an eye out for material. Someday she might get cast as a girl who gets dumped, so how should she play it?

Either way, I don't say a word.

My cell rings. E grabs the phone.

Her voice is a cat scratch over the line:

"She's not home. You're still at the show?"

Pause.

"She's out with friends . . . well, one special friend."

Pause.

"A new guy she met. . . . Heathcliff fell hard for Jess. And she's ready for someone who knows how to appreciate her."

Pause.

"It means what it means."

Pause.

"Don't call back. No one here wants to talk to you."

Pause.

"Creep."

The "creep" part she saves till after she clicks off.

Weirdly, just one dumb idea swirls around in my mind: *Heathcliff* ? Could that name sound more made up?

I didn't think so.

scene 3

For some reason, the sun is shining this morning. Palm trees are swaying in the breeze. Birds are singing.

Stupid birds.

Clearly, the big memo was not as widely distributed as I'd thought. Did you get it? It said: "Jeremy is a two-timer. Life as we lived it is over." I read it all night long.

So much for my sleuthability: I never had a clue.

One thought focuses my fuzzy, sleep-deprived brain: I can't go to Mexico. It's the country that will have Jeremy Jones in it.

I approach Mom in the library. Her checkbook is open and she is looking over some receipts.

"Mom?"

Her face softens as she looks at me. "Yes, *m'ija*?"

"I can't go to Mexico." I slump next to her on the couch. She puts her arms around me and squeezes.

"I know you're sad about Jeremy. But you had good reasons for going to Mexico." She gently rocks me, like when I was little. "What about your Spanish class?"

Like *that* was the reason I wanted to go? Is it fair to get my own big fat fib thrown in my face?

"I'll download some language lessons, Mom."

"Jessica, we're going to Mexico. You can't put off what you want to do because of a boy. If you start now . . . Well, you're not going to start now."

"But Mom . . ."

"Jess, you said you *can't* go to Mexico; you didn't say you didn't want to, you said 'can't.' I'm afraid you won't believe you can unless you do."

I'm going to have to go through torture in a foreign land because of one mischosen word! This is the dark side of Mom-as-librarian—it's not all help with book reports and discounts on overdue charges; sometimes it's the painful bite of grammar forcing you into Mexican exile.

Mom continues. "If you've written anything . . . any of your poems . . . I'd be happy to see them."

"Thanks a lot, Mom." I angrily shake off her arm.

"Jess," she calls as I stomp off. I barely hear her last two words to me. "You *can.*"

I can? I can . . . what?

And who cares if I wrote some dumb rhyme?

When I was little, I copied Mom's habit of putting rhymes into our lunch boxes. I used to show all my silly little poems to her. But now? What's the point?

Why did he drop me?
It's simple as can be—
What I meant to him
Wasn't what he meant to me.

Not pretty enough?
Not famous? Not fun?
Now he's with a girl,
Gorgeous as they come.

There are girls
who are prettier—
More cool, and more clever.
But a girl with a better dog?
He'll never find her. Ever.

scene 4

Mom, E, and I are aboard flight 969 from LAX to Cancún. Not even the hot towels they bring for your hands in first class can make me feel better. And I love those towels.

On my iPod are dozens of songs that I just downloaded: LeAnn Rimes. Faith Hill. Tim McGraw. George Jones. I've never listened to country before, but once your heart's been stomped on, songs like "Long Gone Lonesome Blues," "He Stopped Loving Her To-day," and "You've Ruined Red Carpets for Me Forever" start to make a lot more sense. (That last one is an original composition I'm working on.)

And poetry—those stacks of little sentences stand by you in tough times. This is exactly the kind of poetry you need to read as a broken heart:

> *Love—what is love?*
> *A great and aching heart;*
> *Wrung hands; and silence;*
> *And a long despair.*
> *Life—what is life?*
> *Upon a moorland bare*
> *To see love coming and to see love depart.*
>
> *—R. L. Stevenson*

See? Don't you feel worse already?

I've brought a book of poetry for the plane and my summer reading, *To Kill a Mockingbird*. That title packs as much sad as a whole poem, I say.

Mom is asleep in the seat in front of mine. Eva is reading a *Two Sisters* script. Lavender and Murphy sit across the aisle. Is their "love" so strong they can't be separated while Lavvy goes on location for a few days? Or is it the possibility of publicity that has Murphy coming along?

"Missed y'all at the Roosevelt last night," Lavender tells my sister. She means the opposite. "Everybody was there. Jake, Justin, Cameron . . ." *Don't say Julian, don't say Julian.* ". . . Julian." Ouch. The lead singer of Spilt Sugar is my sister's celebrity crush. ". . . And of course Orlando was all over me to appear in his new movie. It's too boringly blockbuster for me, but you know Orlando. Well, *you* don't know Orlando. And I'm beyond tired of everyone asking me about Orlando."

Lavender was going to say "Orlando" about ten more times, but Murphy interrupted. "Yo, good thing he knows you're with me." He has his portable DVD set up to play *Reservoir Dogs*, and keeps fast-forwarding to all the shoot-'em-up parts. From this angle, I can see another of his tattoos, a colorful dragon climbing his neck toward the back of his trucker hat.

Lavender looks at Murphy like he's kidding about her being "taken." But he's not. Do they *both* know this is a fauxmance?

Murphy doesn't get the vibe, and keeps rat-a-tat-talking about the Roosevelt. "Didja know the ghost of Marilyn Monroe shows up in a mirror there? The one that useta hang in her suite."

Lavender smiles right at me. "Now, why didn't y'all make it to the show? Not another skunk?"

Yes. A superskunk.

"No," says Eva.

"The real show was our two costars," Lavender says, watching for my reaction. "Oooh, at first Ah thought it was a kiss for the cameras, but by the end of the night, let me tell y'all—"

"Sorry, Lavender," Eva interrupts, "but I've got to concentrate on this scene. The writers need me to dig deep."

Lavender smirks and ducks back into her magazine.

Is E lying to shut Lavender up? Here's the dialogue she's reading. You be the judge:

```
          LAVENDER
     If Fido was any more of
     a klutz,
     he'd fall off the floor!


          EVA
     Hahahahahahahaha!
```

Roll laugh track.

PAIGE
Can someone lotion my back?

I'm about to drown my sorrows in Diet Coke and iTunes when a scuffle draws my attention. Someone from coach is trying to use a first-class bathroom when the flight attendant apprehends him. She wraps him in low-quality toilet paper and pushes him back through the thin gray curtain as a warning to other discount fliers.

Well . . . she doesn't *literally* wrap him in T.P., but socially, spiritually, he's busted.

Welcome to my world.

The mystery of the boy—that's way too big for me. I have a much better chance of finding out why someone would want to mail a skunk or dye a water tank black.

I'm going to stick to cases I can solve.

I didn't know there were buildings on our planet as large as the Hotel Banks. You can probably see this place from space. "That blue part is the Gulf of Mexico, and the white part is that resort in Cancún." The hotel is being hastily renamed; all the old Casa del Sol nameplates swapped out for the Banks Brothers logo.

A crowd of tourists cheers at the hotel entrance when the van brings Lavender and Eva to the door. "Attack of the fanny packers," mutters Murphy. The enormous sign held by two valets probably has something to do with the number of people: TWO SISTERS STARS ARRIVING HERE AT 1 P.M. STARS STAY AT HOTEL BANKS.

Eva and Lavender do the smiling and signing thing. Murphy hides out under his tugged-low cap and wraparound dark glasses like he's worried about being recognized; but I don't think his show airs in Mexico. People seem to think he just had Lasik surgery.

Mom has a spooked look on her face.

She had this idea that Eva gets so much attention in Hollywood because it's the center of the TV universe. That somehow other places would be more normal. But I guess television *is* the new

70

neighborhood; you can meet someone from across the country and talk about Angelina or Madonna like they were the people who lived next door to both of you.

A hotel manager greets us and directs Mom, me, and E into the lobby; Lavender and Murphy disappear with another suit. I almost wish I had left my sunglasses on. The place looks like a Godiva box—all gold and swirly lettering. Even the staff uniforms are gold polo shirts and pants. (In fact, with his bald head and uniform, the manager looks oddly like a life-sized Oscar.)

"Money can buy everything but good taste," Mom says to herself.

Taste? Who needs good taste when the lobby features a two-story-high diving board with gold-painted models leaping into a large golden pond? Mom hurries us past when it becomes unclear if the models are wearing anything besides paint.

"Do you think MTV shot *Pimp My Lobby* here?" Eva whispers with a smile.

"Oscar" leads us through a maze of corridors and elevators. One benefit of every surface being painted in eye-squintingly bright gold: Celebs like my sister have an excuse to wear their sunglasses inside. The guided tour of arcades, pools, saunas, spas, movie theater, salon, dance club, and five-star restaurants comes to a crashing halt outside E's door.

Mom has a mom moment.

"Now, girls, listen carefully. Minirefrigerators equal maximum prices. There is no reason to pay eight dollars for a small bag of pretzels when you are able to walk to the gift shop and buy one for a fraction of the price. Do you hear me?"

Kindly, the hotel manager pretends that from his distance of five inches away, he can't hear what Mom is saying.

"Yes, Mom," I say. So Eva won't have to.

The manager opens the door.

"Oh," Mom says.

Which doesn't cover it.

The first room of the suite looks out floor-to-ceiling sliding glass doors onto a stretch of perfect white-sand-meets-ocean. A long black sofa and matching chairs face an almost-movie-screen-sized plasma TV, and a baby grand piano.

E and I race around to check out the rest of the place. The bedrooms have huge high beds, the kind that look like you could sail out to sea on them. The bathrooms each have a sunken tub, wall-to-wall mirrors, and first-class stereo systems. The dining room has a strange metal table and stools set—so modern-looking it shouldn't have been invented yet.

When Eva and I head back to the living room, the manager

presents E with a remote control. "Here's a new feature," he says, pushing buttons. Blinds close out the view, and projected on all the walls is a glowing desert vista. "Or if you'd rather go to the mountains . . ." He touches the keypad, and the view becomes cloud-capped mountains overlooking a bubbling creek.

Cool, but is that a weird setup for a room that has an actual, real-life amazing view?

He gestures toward the kitchen. "Fully stocked. Your publicist provided a list of your food requests." He avoids Mom's eye. "All complimentary."

The richer you get, the more people want to give you free stuff. I don't understand that, except that maybe it's the rich people who decide who gets the free stuff?

Mom has barely moved beyond the doorway. Her eyes are taking in the snowcapped peaks, the flowers, the piano, the two-thousand-dollars-a-night-ness of it all. Finally, barely audible over the sound of piped-in creek burbling, she says to E, "But you don't even play the piano."

Every once in a while Mom gets another hit of culture shock. Celebrity can be more of a foreign country than an actual foreign country.

*M*om and Eva get right to unpacking (they declined Oscar's offer to have the housekeepers do it), but the beach is calling my name. It's even pronouncing my name Spanish-style: Hessica. I change into a green tank top, shorts, and sandals.

"Mom, I'm going to the beach. Right outside the door."

"Está bien," she says. Because, you know, I only headed south of the border to work on my Spanish.

Here's what I can tell you about Mexico: The ocean is warm, the beaches are white, and the Mexican food is *fabulous*—even the little burrito bar on the beach is serving up pita-wrapped slices of heaven. The virgin margaritas alone are enough to layer a thin spread of happy over my deep base of misery.

You might have guessed this, but let me confirm: Having my heart stomped, on national television, by my cheating, first-ever almost-boyfriend, post-perfect-kiss, is a bad thing. But there is one thing worse than heart stompage: turning into a Sad Hoper. You know—the girl who holds on to some ridiculous dream that the guy who doesn't care suddenly will.

The best thing to do is concentrate my full attention on stopping the set saboteur before Murphy—oops, I mean, before *he or she*—strikes again.

I'm looking for motive, means, and opportunity.

And I know where to start.

$$\star$$

Theoretically.

In theory, I know where to start.

In reality, I don't know where to look for Murphy and Lavender. How can I find anyone in this place? Pink walls overly accented with gold, white tile floors, and German tourists: the hotel hallways are all decorated the same.

I hang out in the lobby for a bit. How can I find . . . ?

"Move it! Move IT! MOVE it!"

Murphy is around the corner and halfway down the hall, but the guy's voice carries. He is plowing through tourists and staff with a pink plaid travel bag swung over his shoulder. And with me in pursuit. He is wearing jeans, a faded concert T-shirt, and that seriously post-trend trucker hat. He turns down a corridor into a conference room.

Hmmm . . . bad boys don't do plaid. And it can't be Lavender's bag because it's not, you know, *lavender*. What's up?

Standing outside the door Murphy entered, I hear a familiar voice: "Friends, Roman, countrymen . . . I was sure that was funny."

"Al, please?" Amber's voice. "Could we get back to the story? Roman is going to unravel the strands of my DNA if we don't get something together fast."

The writers are at work.

"Unravel the strands?" Al sounds thoughtful. "Not funny."

Other voices chime in. "Agree." "Not funny." "Thumbs down."

Amber's voice rises. "Agreed! Not funny! Especially to me, the unravel-ee, so let's get to reworking the story line. We want to take better advantage of the new location."

Translation: They want more excuses to put the cast in bathing suits. There's a reason so many reality shows are shot in hot locations. It's called the bikini factor. The producers don't want the babes bundled up in snowsuits.

Peeking through the door, I see the writing staff gathered around a long wooden conference table. Huge white poster boards are set up all over the room. The posters are scrawled with story ideas. Most of the ideas have big Xs through them.

The room buzzes with energy. You know that kid in class whose hand shoots up for every answer? This place is packed with "pick me!" kids.

At the back of the room, a bamboo screen conceals a snack spread. Murphy is peering around the screen at the writers.

I text E because Mom might be looking for me by now. Then I push open the door. It creaks and Murphy shoots me a look. He presses a finger to his lips: Don't interrupt the eavesdropping.

I hear one of the junior writers tell Amber, "There's only one problem with your plotline: it sucks all the funny out of the story and leaves behind a rotting carcass of unwatchable, ratings-killing drek!"

Yikes. And I thought getting a bad grade was hard.

Murphy tugs at his trucker hat—it says *Crank Pranksters* across the back; the front features a black button, like an empty eye. He carefully removes the hat, tucking it under his arm, and I get my first close-up look at him. With the brown eyes, wide mouth, and broad cheekbones, the guy should be dangerously good-looking— except that he's dared to take on the fashion gods.

And they have not been merciful.

That's right: white-man cornrows.

I don't know why it's wrong; I only know that it is.

So wrong.

Murphy smirks at the tension in the room. "Writers are just heart attacks in cheap jeans and baseball caps." Lucky for him the writers are now shouting at one another so even his voice is drowned out. He picks over the fruit tray beside me. "What're you doin' here?"

"I got lost." Technically, true. I have no idea where this room is. "What are *you* doing here?"

He narrows his eyes. "Nosy, aren't you?" From the guy who had his face pressed to the gap in the bamboo screen. "I was trying to return this to that preppy geek." He kicks the plaid bag at his feet. "The porters mixed it up with my stuff. But Brooks Brothers isn't here."

Then he shrugs and walks out, leaving the bag behind. I look at it. Will one of the other writers return it to Carlton?

Amber's voice rises above the rest: "You're all overeducated monkey minds who wouldn't know a good idea if it bit you on the . . ."

Hmmm . . . maybe I better return it myself. I hurry out of the writers' room, but can't quite place where I am. I turn down one hallway, then another, then another. Till I find myself in the smack-dab center of the Worst Place on the Planet.

*D*on't be fooled by the rocking music, happy crowd, and enormous dance floor spilling onto the beach. The Baila Beach Club of the Hotel Banks is officially the Worst Place on the Planet. You might have thought the worst place was the North Pole in sunless January, or where those ten-foot tubeworms grow near boiling undersea vents, or maybe the Chanel sample sale when you're reaching for the same mauve ballet flats as Lavender.

But you'd be wrong.

The Baila is the worst place because it's the place where Jeremy Jones is. Right now.

The last time he looked at me, he was smiling.

Now he is looking at me like I am a stranger. Which doesn't feel good.

He's incredibly handsome in his blue-brings-out-my-eyes T-shirt and shorts. Which feels worse.

"Hello, Jessica," he says coolly.

I want to say something calm, yet cutting. Startle him with my sophistication and aplomb. What I come up with is: "Hello, Jeremy."

Scriptwriters are never around when you *really* need them.

All around us, people are *bailando* in their bathing suits and having a great time; we're an island of angry.

Jeremy looks at me for a long moment. The DJ pumps up the music, so Jeremy winds up half-shouting in my ear. "I don't know why you're making that . . . *huffy-puffy* face at me."

First off, I'm making a *fierce* face to inspire fear and trembling, *not* a huffy-puffy face. And second off . . . "Like you don't know?"

For an instant, Jeremy looks truly angry, like I've never seen him. I take a step back without meaning to, and—*ouch!* Some girl salsas into my back. "You hook up with some guy, and not only do I get ripped . . . by your *sister* . . . over the *phone* . . . but then I get dagger eyes from you?"

The DJ yells something that sounds like "foam cannon," but that doesn't make any sense. And neither does what Jeremy just said.

My jaw must be slamming the ground like a cartoon character's. "What? The first thing that happened, before . . ." What was the name? *What was the name?* ". . . Heathcliff and I got together was that I saw you making out with Paige on national television."

Jeremy looks startled. "And what . . . ? You forgot that TV isn't real life?"

"Foam! Foam!" the crowd shouts. *"Foam! Foam!"*

I don't know what to say. Was Jeremy not interested in Paige?

But he let the reporter (and the United States of America, including my *abuela*) believe he was. Even my mom and sister assumed he'd dropped me. And who wouldn't want a beautiful model–TV star over me? Maybe Jeremy . . . ?

At that moment, DJs step behind little cannons and spray the place with hundreds of gallons of foam! In seconds, I'm knee-deep and the crowd is dancing and tossing foam around like crazy.

I feel like jumping up and down too, but it has nothing to do with the music. Hope is exploding inside me like, well, a foam cannon. When suddenly . . .

FIZZLE

"Oh, *Remy*, there you are, darling!" Paige appears between us and throws her arms around Jeremy. Her long nails flash with little suns, clawing his shoulders. In heels, she's almost his height exactly. Her famous ash-blond hair coils past her shoulders.

For a minute, Jeremy looks at me over Paige's shoulder as she latches on to him like a screamer monkey. He seems almost . . .

miserable. But that is the problem with every actor. You don't know when he's, you know, *acting*.

I throw Carlton's bag over my shoulder and start wading through waist-deep foam into the crowd.

I'm getting out of here before the day can get any worse.

Exiting, one of the dancing guys steps on my foot, then feels the need to tell me, "Can you believe that Señorita Paige is here? She's *muy caliente*."

Just.

Got.

Worse.

I pick up a hotel map from the lobby. It takes the clerk a while to find Carlton's room number, but then I'm on my way into one of the gleaming gold-and-dark-wood elevators. A tall woman in an outrageously touristy outfit joins me. She hasn't missed a mark on the bad-taste checklist: Birkenstocks with white socks, fluorescent flowered muumuu, enormous floppy hat, face-covering sunglasses, and pounds of plastic bracelets clicking over her folded hands.

Maybe I'm grasping at any non-Jeremy thought, but my brain bubbles with the question: who looks in the mirror and thinks Birks, bangles, blanket dress, let's roll?

Or is she a victim of the ever-changing world of fashion? Two words explain why Mom doesn't let us look at her old yearbooks: *Big. Hair.*

I'd love to know what Ms. Muu thinks. But then how would I feel if I show up at my new Beverly Hills high school (in less than two months!), and the girls treat my old Anaheim life like a cultural curiosity?

I think of a rhyme I wrote. Another one that I'll never show my mother.

New girl in a brand-new world.
Moved from home, shaken and swirled.
"Where's she from? What's she done?
If we have a party, do we want her to come?
"Out of Anaheim? That's not like us.
Can't ride a horse. She rides a bus.

Not even a butler standing at her door?
If you ring the bell, then what's in store?"

The elevator rings for tourist-woman's floor, and she exits. Alone, I can't resist the chance to peek at Carlton's bag. It's hanging open.

Really.

Truly.

This is fully a coincidence.

The zipper happens to be partly open. Allowing a peek inside.

I squat beside the bag. Resting on top of all the perfectly folded khaki is a piece of paper, practically crying out: "Read me, Jessica!"

I have to stop the crying.

The paper is a pitch for a new television show. The name? *Skunk'd*.

You know what it's about: setting skunks after celebrities. The skunks would have minicameras attached to their collars. Just when I thought they couldn't make cameras any smaller, or weirder.

I'm digging through the bag when the elevator rings for my floor. The doors open and I look up to see . . . did I mention that I have really bad luck?

"**W**hat are you doing?"

Carlton is not happy to find me rooting through his personal belongings.

I play it cool, coming up with a fast plan. "I found this bag. I was looking to see who it belongs to."

That's right—me and ice cream, we're both s-m-o-o-t-h.

Carlton looms over me as I stand up. He presses against one of the elevator doors to hold it open. "That's my bag."

"Oh?" *Imagine my surprise . . .*

"Isn't it obvious?" At first, I think he means because the bag looks like a page out of a preppy handbook, but when Carlton reaches out to grab it from my hands, I see that the name C-A-R-L-T-O-N has been embroidered in huge letters on the side.

Like ice cream, I'm melting.

"There are lots of Carltons in . . . Mexico." Okay, that would probably sound more likely if we were in Connecticut, not Cancún.

"It was stolen out of the van," he says.

"Stolen?"

He's a cool customer too. Now he can deny that the *Skunk'd* proposal is his. "Look, Carlton, can I ask you . . . ?"

"No. You can't." He steps back from the doors, letting them slide shut. I can't read the last expression on his face: suspicion? Or worry?

The next morning, the sun wakes me in my bed. Which for an L.A. girl is a new experience. In Mexico, it doesn't take all morning for the smog to burn off. Cancún starts every day in full color.

The full-strength morning light gets me up—and so does the sound of a small army stomping around the living room. I change my pj's for a T-shirt and cutoffs, and head out to see what the noise is about. Everyone is talking—except for Mom. She is staring straight ahead.

It's busy at the suite—the first day of shooting—but Mom's frozen freak-out mode is not comforting.

Here's the scene: Steve is flat-ironing Eva's hair. One assistant is giving E a manicure; another is providing a pedicure. Mary has more equipment spread around than an air traffic controller: mirrors, eye shadow palettes, brushes of every size. Hélène is waiting to give E her fitting, so she is passing time playing the piano.

Mom pastes on a smile. "Someone is using the piano," she says dazedly. "Isn't that nice?"

Eva takes in Mom's blank face. "Mom, do you want to use my appointment with the masseuse? You look stressed."

"No, thank you, *m'ija*." Mom is pulling herself together. "I know where to go for help." She's either talking about the Bible or some other big book, but she appears so much calmer I'm almost glad to know that she'll be off working up some life lesson for us. "I'm going to do some research online in the other room. Please call me when it's time to leave for the set."

Steve irons Eva's locks into perfect smoothness. Mary applies moisturizer.

"Where are you shooting today, E?"

"Chichén Itzá. Ancient Mayan pyramids and ruins."

"Cool."

"Yeah, it's a party scene to celebrate rescuing Mr. Ruffs from the petnappers." Because nothing says "welcome back" like a visit to the site of ancient ritual sacrifice. The cast hasn't even shot the rescue that they'll be celebrating. On location, *Two Sisters* is shot out of sequence, according to what area is prepped.

Steve's phone buzzes. He checks. "It's a text from Roman, we're leaving in five."

As Hélène is helping E into her outfit for the scene (yellow flutter-sleeve wrap top and green prairie skirt), I have a chance to ask E a question: "Could Carlton be writing for another show?"

Eva raises an eyebrow. "Ambitious writers always have something going beside their main job. Pitching new shows. Writing movies. Remember that Ahmed guy who used to work for Al? He quit to adapt some Jane Austen novel for Dreamworks." Eva sighs. "I wish I had gotten to know him better."

Now that he's influential.

"E, how would I find out if a new TV show was being shopped around?"

"Carlton is writing a new show?"

Before I can explain, Mom appears, wearing a big smile. Too big. "I think I'm on to something, girls. We don't want flattery, fluffing, and free gifts to get to us, right?"

Eva and I look at each other. What's the right answer here?

"No?" offers E. Hélène is at her feet, strapping on sandals. "No, we don't?"

"Of course not! So I've ordered some books that are going to help set up a new program for us."

No! Please don't slam the swag!

Some of the clothes that come for E are too small for me, but the phones, handbags, jewelry—that's one-sister-fits-all. Take the flattery and fluffing, and go in peace. But have mercy on the free products.

Eva nods. This could be serious, but E's mind is elsewhere. I don't realize where until we get to the lobby.

Then I'm surprised. But maybe I shouldn't be.

scene 8

Cast and crew gather in the lobby. Eva, Mom, and I are being shown into a Range Rover when E spots the person she's been looking for.

(Thankfully the person I'm looking for doesn't seem to be around. He might already be shooting at Chichén Itzá.)

"Carlton!" E calls.

I hadn't noticed Carlton at first because he is sporting a new, seriously bad haircut. He must know it too, because he touches his too-short white-blond crew cut and says, "I asked the hotel barber for a Caesar."

Yikes. The barber must have thought he said a "Simpson"—as in Homer. Such are the problems of translation in a foreign land.

"Looks cool," says Eva. Carlton brightens. *Whoa,* sister-girl can act. She smiles. "You should ride with us."

"I should?"

"C'mon."

Mom watches Carlton closely as he waves off Amber and the other writers, and steps into the Range Rover.

"I'm Carlton, Mrs. Ortiz." He extends his hand formally for a shake.

"Yes, I know." She gives him an appraising look, trying to figure out why Carlton is here. But it's clear that he has no clue either.

Mom sits up front next to the driver. She keeps an eye on the rearview mirror—and Carlton—while she calls in to the set.

As the SUV pulls away, Eva starts quizzing Carlton. "The writers are working hard on the Mexico scenes, right?"

Carlton rubs his glasses on his shirt. His pinched face takes on a gleam as he talks about his work. "Absolutely. We have twenty-one minutes to tell a great story. It's not about filling the gap between fast-food commercials. Am I right?"

Mmm . . . french fries. Extra-salty.

Oops. Must concentrate.

"So true," agrees Eva. "Have *you* come up with any ideas lately?"

"I've been pitching this idea for next season that's a takeoff on the *Ring* movies."

"Sounds fantastic!" What? E didn't want to see *Mean Girls* because she thought it sounded harsh; now she's a killer-videotape fan? "Copying a big movie—so original."

Carlton looks closely at E. "You know, Eva, you've got some of that Naomi Watts thing going on."

This may be the first time a Mexican American girl has *ever* been told this. My sister gets the Jessica Alba thing and the occasional J.Lo thing, but the blue-eyed, blond Australian thing? Not so much.

"You think?" Eva asks.

"Absolutely. I had her in mind for this spec movie I'm writing, but you would be such a better fit." A spec movie is one that a writer isn't paid to create; he's home alone pounding his computer, hoping for his big break.

"I'd love to read it," says E. "Anything *else* you're writing?"

At this point, I don't know who is playing whom. But I'm sure E wouldn't be smiling like that if she knew the show he's pitching was *Skunk'd*.

Carlton says, "Coming up with ideas isn't easy. Sometimes people think they have a great idea for a show—and will do pretty strange things to get attention—and it turns out the idea stinks." What is he talking about? And why is he looking at me?

Before Eva can respond, her phone beeps. "Text from Keiko.

She's sending me a Mason Pearson hairbrush. *InStyle* is doing an article on how Angelina and Beyoncé swear by them."

"Ha!" Mom says from the front seat. "If I paid one hundred dollars for a hairbrush, I'd be swearing, too."

And then she really does.

Swear, that is.

"Cripes" is a swearword in Mom-land.

Her cell phone has beeped with bad news. She turns around from the front seat, looking worried. "There's been more trouble on the set." She frowns. "But what they've taken makes no sense."

Carlton squeezes my hand briefly. "Don't worry, Jessica," he says in a low voice. "I can be your alibi."

I stare at him. It's strange when you don't know whether to give someone your thanks—or your elbow, right under the Izod-covered ribs.

Act
III

Boys frustrate me. I hate all their indirect messages.
I hate game playing. Do you like me or don't you?
Just tell me so I can get over you.

—KIRSTEN DUNST

For the obvious reasons, ruins of a once-great civilization are right up there with poetry and country music on the approved-for-broken-hearts list.

The sun is beating down as we emerge into a mass of tourists. Mom helps Eva navigate the crowd; the librarian in Mom looks vaguely depressed that people would rather take photos of a TV teenager than thousand-year-old temples.

A guide greets us, leading the way through the stone corridors to the *Two Sisters* shooting area. The black, gray, and white stone contrasts with the rainbow of greens on display in the creeping jungle. The guide explains that the ancient Mayans invented the calendars we use today, mapped the stars, and were masters of mathematics. Without metal tools or the wheel, they built vast cities across the jungles.

For a girl from L.A., where "old" is any building that doesn't have air-conditioning, the sight of the massive stone pyramid, El Castillo, is amazing. It must be a slow climb to the top because the steps are only deep enough to fit the front part of your foot.

The guide implies that this was to keep the human sacrifices from being able to run away. If he's saying that to freak out the American girl . . . it works.

The *Two Sisters* crew is freaked out too. There was a theft at the prop tent.

Eduardo, the local property master, suspects it was a souvenir-seeking tourist. He is a gray-haired, grandfatherly type. "All the thief took was the gift-wrapped packages for the party scene. The boxes looked fancy, but they were empty props. Nothing valuable."

"They were valuable to *us,* babe," growls Roman. Eduardo's attempt to talk himself out of trouble doesn't fly. Roman turns to his head writer. "Al, what are we going to do?"

Anxious Al squeezes his hands together. The eye twitch he's developed isn't comforting either. "Give me a minute, Roman. . . ."

"We don't have a minute!" Roman barks. "The crew is here *this* minute. On the clock." Roman turns to Carlton. "Quick Carlton?"

Amber interrupts before Carlton can say a word. Her stomping on his penny loafers might have slowed him down a notch. "We just need a bunch of presents, and this place has a gift shop. Maybe Eduardo could run over there?"

Roman nods. "Eduardo, you'll make this right, yes?"

"*Sí.* I will need help carrying the packages to make it in one trip."

Mom presses my shoulder. "Jessica would be happy to help carry the packages, Eduardo."

Eduardo smiles at me. *"Gracias."* We head to the gift shop. "Is Señor Roman always like that?" he asks.

"Yeah, he usually acts like his hair is on fire."

"And his bottom, too." Eduardo relaxes with every step away from Roman. "Many U.S. shows film here, but I have never had problems before." We approach the gift shop and Eduardo whispers, "Keep an eye out for any lights they might be selling. I did not get a chance to tell Roman, but a string of the party lights was taken too."

Empty packages? Colored lights? Is this sabotage related to the skunking? To the ink-out? Or just the work of greedy tourists?

Eduardo gets the shop to sell him gift-wrapped empty boxes. I can't find any electrical lights, but there are some candles, and tiki-type candleholders.

"And look what I found." Eduardo hands me a leather bracelet. It has El Castillo pictured on it, along with the name Jessica stenciled in dark letters.

"Gracias, Eduardo."

His brown eyes crinkle with his smile. Sometimes people are lovely just because they feel a human connection.

"Perhaps you could get Eva's signature for me? My daughter is a fan."

"Sure."

I don't feel like he bought my sister's autograph.

I don't.

⭐

The crew is getting all the props in place. Eva is running lines with Mom, and I'm keeping an eye out for Murphy. I see Lavender, but not her cornrowed boyfriend. Did he disappear before the theft? Or after?

Since you know Lavender is tall, skinny, and a former Miss Teen Sensation—that is, gorgeous—you might be surprised to know why she has a black marker in hand as she reviews her publicity photos. She is noting which of her features she wants airbrushed. She marks where she wants the whites of her eyes and her teeth brightened—quicker than Crest White Strips.

There is a bustle from the surrounding tourists when the other two members of the cast join us. We can see the two blond heads pausing for autographs among the crowd. I don't want to be here, seeing Paige and Jeremy together. But I have to admit I'm curious to see how my sister will take on the costars she thinks have wronged me. She'll either be fake-friendly . . .

"Please tell Paige to stay out of my lighting," announces Eva. "Her hips cast quite a shadow."

Or not fake-friendly.

There is a stir of excitement as Paige arrives. Jeremy trails behind her. Paige is spangly with oversized jewelry, and her clothes have more labels than a spice rack. Louis Vuitton pants; Marc Jacobs shirt under a Chanel jacket; Manolo Blahnik shoes; and an enormous Coach bag.

Eva moves closer to me, putting her body between me and the new couple. She whispers: "All that's missing is the label that says, 'I'm a poser with too much money.'"

Then Eva moves toward Paige and Jeremy. Jeremy looks concerned. He's no fool. Paige, on the other hand . . . beams at my sister and starts barking. Three startled little yips.

"Is there a dog here?" Eva asks, confused.

"Here's my new puppy," says Paige, gaily whipping a scrawny mass of fur and anxiety out of her oversized purse. A tuft of white hair perches on top of the dog's head; otherwise his naked-looking body is shivery and pink. "Isn't he superfab? He came with the bag."

Eva blinks. "The bag?"

"His name is Tinkles. Get it? I introduce him as 'my dog Tinkles.' Funny, huh?"

Say what, now?

Jeremy's taste in girlfriends is a little suspect—one of the main things I had in my favor. But for him to rain all over my "kiss-zing" memories for "my dog Tinkles"? Does this make sense to you?

Jeremy is not looking at me—or anyone. He stares at the ground during the whole horrible Tinkling.

Paige is still smiling at my sister. "What about that dog you have, Eva? Is he a Coach or Louis Vuitton?"

Eva stares at Paige. She looks like she is trying to decide between quick physical revenge and slow psychological torture.

Jeremy cuts in quickly, "You met Petunia, Paige. She's an English bulldog."

She looks puzzled. "English Bulldog? Is that Stella McCartney's new line?"

Paige was actually making more sense when I thought she was yipping.

Paige notices me staring, and gives me a split-second appraisal. The look on her face says, "No competition." Then she runs five sun-painted fingernails along Jeremy's cheek. The cameras weren't rolling, but my stomach was.

Jeremy starts to pull Paige away. He doesn't take her hand; he tugs on her sleeve. "Let's go, Paige."

Before the two can get away, Tommy "Pet-Man" Peterson arrives with this episode's animal costar, Mr. Ruffs, gathered in his arms. Now here is a dog. He is a brown cocker spaniel mix. So cute. "Did I hear another dog on set?"

"My dog Tinkles," Paige says, giggling.

Tommy looks worried. "Are you thinking of training Tinkles as an actor?"

"I hadn't thought of it, Pet-Man." Paige looks him over with her puddly green eyes. "Till you mentioned it." Tommy gets red in the face and stalks off clutching Mr. Ruffs. He shouldn't worry about the competition: Tink is purely a fashion accessory.

Roman arrives to welcome Paige and Jeremy. "Good scene you shot earlier. Nice chemistry. Maybe we can get you to play romantic partners on the show as well as in real life?"

Paige smiles. "Great idea. I'm always happy to pitch in." She grips Roman's arm urgently. "We all have to work together to make the magic happen. We're like a relay team. No one player can carry the baton."

Roman wrestles his arm free. "Okay, then." Pause. "Maybe the writers can work something in—they're getting used to last-minute revisions."

Nothing could make the moment worse . . . except for the sweet, syncopated rhythms of Gwen Stefani as my cell phone goes off.

Jeremy and I get caught in a quick shared glance. I begin to pull my phone from my pocket, when I realize from the stricken look on Jeremy's face that it could be *his* phone. Neither of us moves.

The song goes on.

The planets turn.

New species evolve.

Stars are born and burn out.

After an eternity or ten, my (or Jeremy's) phone stops ringing.

Then another cell phone chirps. "That's me!" trills Paige. She pops her phone open and even from where I'm standing, I can hear angry squawking coming through the line.

Paige cuts off the caller: "What's your man got to do with me? I got a man!"

Click! She flips off the cell phone and smiles brightly. "Wrong number."

I have to wonder: do you have to be crazy to get into the acting business?

If it's not mandatory, it is one *huge* coincidence.

Mom has stepped beside me. She wraps a warm arm around my shoulders. "Want to see something terrible?" she whispers in her keeping-secrets voice.

But I already *am* seeing something terrible: Paige reaching for Jeremy's hand, and holding on. Tight.

scene 2

When given the choice of watching Paige smooch up Jeremy, or visiting the site of ancient ritual sacrifices, well, I had to go with the less horrifying option.

Mom and I look out over a green pond surrounded by layers of stones. A guide is saying, "The Mayans prized the Sacred Well for its religious significance. Warriors were thrown in alive as an offering to the god of water in times of drought. They believed that the men did not die, even though they were not seen again."

Brr . . .

"And you fought me on those swimming lessons," Mom says in a low voice. We follow the crowd to the Ball Court, a huge playing field with a small temple at each end. The guide explains, "The game involved two teams hitting the ball with only elbows, wrists, or hips. The goal was to knock the ball through one of the stone hoops on the walls of the court."

A peek at the stone carvings on the court wall shows that the Mayans weren't playing for bragging rights: one team member has blood spurting from his headless neck, while another holds the head aloft.

Double brr . . .

Mom slips away to the far end of the court, and takes out her cell. The Mayans must have been acoustic wizards because I can clearly hear what she's saying.

And it's clear she doesn't know it. "Rob, one daughter gets broken up with via national television; the other has her every whim anticipated. There are people who make up things for Eva to want. But I think I've finally found some reference for this." Mom went to school to become the kind of person who is absurdly delighted to help people discover the top exports of Belize—so the lack of parenting manuals related to TV star teens and their less accomplished sisters has been disorienting for her. "And how did that Jones boy get past my radar? I count on being able to peg the bad guys. I tell you, Rob, these slick Hollywood kids have me second-guessing myself."

Mom is beating herself up for misjudging Jeremy. Dad must

share his own viewpoint because she answers him: "No, Robert, you can't kick his butt."

The Way of the Dad is simple, and almost always embarrassing and inappropriate. It must be the exposure to a more primitive culture because—for one small moment—I really appreciate his offer.

Beside me the guide is explaining to our group, "Words softly spoken at the other end of the court, over five hundred feet away, are clearly audible at our end. Researchers have tried to explain how this is possible—they'd hoped to apply the acoustic principles to all open-air theaters—but to this day it has not been explained."

Some mysteries weren't meant to be solved.

Mom rejoins me. Neither of us mentions her call.

The guide next leads us to El Castillo, announcing, "Each side of the pyramid originally had ninety-one steps. Counting the platform at the top as a final step, there are three hundred and sixty-five in all—matching the days of the year. At the spring and autumn equinoxes, the shadow of the sun against the stairs creates the illusion of an enormous snake moving down the pyramid toward the Sacred Well."

The Mayans knew how to create chills even in the heat of the day.

I'm surprised to see a tall woman in Birks and a bright pink muumuu. I can't see her face—it's shielded by the enormous hat and glasses—but it must be the same tourist from the hotel, right? There couldn't be two of those outfits in the world. She heads off to the Sacred Well, and all I can think is: that outfit is something that should be sacrificed.

Mom and I make our way slowly to the top. We look out over the plaza of crumbling stone temples and creeping jungle. Mom sits down while I make my way around the side of the pyramid, and hear: "Carlton—that preppy little phony."

It's Murphy. He *did* come to Chichén Itzá. But did he arrive before the theft or after? Under his bulky *Crank Pranksters* cap, Murphy looks through binoculars toward the shoot.

He doesn't notice me till I'm right beside him. He's wearing a green T-shirt and jeans. His clothes come in only one size: tight.

I tap his shoulder.

"Whaddaya want?" he asks, loud and angry. I can't tell if he's unhappy to see me, or just being a New Yorker.

"I was wondering where you were"—here goes—"when the props were stolen this morning."

Murphy gives me a cold look, and I get a sudden real-time sense of the history of violence at El Castillo. I creep back from the edge of the terrace. "That your idea of a *subtle* question?"

Sadly, yes.

He scowls. "I was watching Paige and Jeremy shoot some scene. Bob and I split an *empanada*—if you want *proof*."

He wraps the straps of his binoculars around his neck and starts to head down the steps. I follow him. We're both moving awkwardly; the short steps require a funny, sideways movement. *Hop-hop*-steady-steady. We must look like part of Mexico's most ridiculous chase scene.

"So you don't know anything about the inking, either?" I call after him. "Or skunking?"

Murphy doesn't look back. He leaps off the bottom steps, and stomps away.

Not my most successful suspect interrogation.

Still, I feel like myself for the first time since the fashion show. I'm on a case, working the clues, helping the team. I'm me again—totally over Jeremy Jones.

I mean, Jeremy who?

I mean, who who?

Bothered by who who? Who, me?

$\mathcal{E}$va and I awake the next morning to find Mom happily settled in on the living room couch. There's a thick hardcover book on her lap, and several more piled around her.

"I've found some relevant parenting books," she says brightly.

Really? Can you picture these books on the bestseller list? *What to Expect When You're Expecting a TV Star; Your Child, Your Chance: Living Vicariously Through Your Daughter;* and *Ways to Stunt Your Child Actor's Growth: Cut Out the Calcium and More!*

Basically, Mom tortures herself wondering if she ever should have let Eva get into the business. But it's pretty clear to me that if Eva didn't have acting as an outlet, she'd be . . . well . . . Abuela.

"There aren't any guides for parents of actors, but top athletes lead very similar lives."

Eva looks wary. "What's the name of that book, Mom?"

Mom puts her book down. It sinks so far into the sofa, it must weigh more than a small child. I read the title: *Thin Ice: How the*

Demands of Championship Figure Skating Can Scare and Scar Your Daughter. Forever.

Two words come to mind: *Uh. Oh.*

"Mom, I'm not scarred or scared," Eva says. "It's acting that I love, not all the baggage that comes with it."

Mom nods encouragingly. "Very good, Eva. I give you a seven for self-expression."

"You're giving me seven . . . what?"

"I'm giving you a seven—a positive, but not inflated, rating of your response." Mom looks at me. "Now, Jess, I haven't found any books about the siblings of athletes, but I'm looking."

Joy.

Eva, knowing it's futile to resist when Mom is determined to help her, has to try anyway: "Mom, I know you're working hard at this. . . ."

"Well, thank you, *m'ija*. Give yourself an eight for empathy."

Mom heads for the kitchen. Eva looks at me, and I whisper, "Are you thinking that Mom . . ."

". . . gets a ten for crazy?" Eva whispers back. "Yep, that's what I'm thinking."

*E*va and I sit out on the beach together in tank tops, shorts, and flip-flops. The Mexican sun is deliciously hot on my skin, and I drink greedily from my bottle of water. We're propped on beach chairs next to each other, but I know that our thoughts are buzzing on different paths.

I'd bet my one pair of perfectly fitting jeans that Eva is thinking about the theft at Chichén Itzá—if Amber hadn't thought to substitute in new gifts, the scene would have been rewritten, with E's part cut down. Again.

I'm trying to piece together the clues to Project Stop Skunk.

The skunk arrived at our house timed perfectly for the *TRL* interview, marked with an official *Two Sisters* label, and bearing the name of Eva's boss. Later, a *Skunk'd* TV proposal appears in Carlton's "stolen" bag. Result: less airtime for Eva. And a trial run for Carlton's new TV show?

The water tank was damaged just enough to kill the day's shoot. A witness puts a person with a red jacket and ponytail at the scene. Lavender convinced Roman not to call the police. What did she say? Was she protecting her pranky boyfriend? Then again, *she's* one of the people with long brown hair around here. Result: Carlton saves the day. Less airtime for Eva and Lavender. More airtime for Jeremy and Paige.

The stolen gifts and lights: the work of random thievery? Result: Eduardo gets in trouble. More money spent at gift shop. Airtime remains the same. I still need to check with Lighting Guy Bob to see if Murphy was with him.

E lifts her head out of her script. She watches me scribbling in the sand. "Dad makes the best . . ."

"Yeah, he does." Dad is an expert mechanic with his own garage in Anaheim. We were the kids with the most elaborate forts, turrets, and moats decorating our sand castles. Our tree house had a working pulley system for milk-and-cookie deliveries. I think Eva got cast in her first plays because the theaters wanted Dad's help with the stagecraft.

"Remember that time . . . ?"

"Yeah."

"Me too."

I draw a little figure in the sand. Big belly, big smile.

"You must be missing . . ." For a minute, I think she means Jeremy. I freeze. Then I realize who I really am missing. Petunia.

"Yeah, I am."

"Maybe you could visit with Mr. Ruffs? Tide you over?"

"Great idea!"

I'm impressed that E would be tuned in to how much I'm

missing Petunia. Don't get me wrong. I love E and she loves me. How many people can you pick up conversations with in the middle of a sentence and know what they are thinking? Who else has the history?

But the thoughtfulness? Not always E's defining quality. The flip side of her focus, I guess.

So I shouldn't feel surprised to see that her Mr. Ruffs idea serves another purpose: getting rid of me.

I shouldn't feel surprised when I see Carlton. But I do.

His khakis are rolled to the knee, and he carries a pair of Docksiders and a straw hat as he walks across the beach. His face is as pink as his polo.

"Hi, Carlton!" I see that he has script pages tucked clumsily under his arm.

My sister smiles at Carlton—a bright, is-she-acting-or-not? grin. Then she makes a small gesture, pulling on her earring. It might not have been a conscious gesture, but I am suddenly sure that our Just Go signal has been translated into a Just Leave signal.

And so I do. It's time for puppy love.

Let's hope I'm talking about myself—not my sister!

ommy and Mr. Ruffs are staying in the farthest possible corner of the hotel. I have to keep checking the hotel map to find them. By the time I arrive outside the door, I'm not sure I'm still in Mexico anymore.

Tommy answers my knock. "Jessica, right?"

"Yes, hello. I was wondering if I could visit with Mr. Ruffs. I miss my own dog, Petunia. She's an English bulldog—"

"Sorry, Jessica. I'm going for a swim, and Mr. Ruffs can't have any visitors right now. He's preparing for his big scene."

Preparing?

I hear Mr. Ruffs barking in the background. I know a plaintive, come-play-with-me bark when I hear it. Tommy says goodbye, and the door locks behind him as he heads down the corridor.

I should go back to my room.

I should not bother the hardworking housekeeper rounding the corner.

And I almost don't, except something about her sharp brown eyes reminds me of Abuela, and I smile at her. She smiles back. Her name tag says Rita.

"*Habla inglés,* Rita?"

"A little."

Can I do this? Should I do this?

How-oo!

Mr. Ruffs howls his lonely cry again. I only want to help—but does that make it right? Rita is still looking at me.

I push aside the sticky-guilties.

"My key card isn't working on my door." I can't meet her eye as I flash my own room card. They all look alike in the hotel—plastic rectangles with the Hotel Banks crest. "My dog—*mi perro*—needs me. Could you . . ."

"*Ay, niña!* Okay. Okay."

"*Gracias, gracias.*" She opens the door, then rolls off with her cart as I enter the dark room. Tommy's room is the size of E's kitchen, with one double bed, a sliding door opening onto a courtyard, and a tiny bathroom. I suspect the food in his mini-fridge is not complimentary.

I flip on the lights. Mr. Ruffs is in his cage. His tail is thumping the hard cage walls.

Can't have that, right?

I lift the bar on his cage and twenty pounds of happy cocker spaniel tumbles into my arms. He sniffs at my clothes, tail wagging. Then he discovers the Jessica bracelet looped around my wrist—a new chew toy.

We're just playing with his toys and being silly and having fun. He doesn't even ask for an autograph. We're having such a good time that I don't know how much later it is that I hear the door handle jiggle.

I freeze, and then hurry Mr. Ruffs back into his cage, trying to ignore his "come and play" whine. I hit the lights and sneak out the sliding glass door onto the courtyard. The light comes back on in the room behind me.

A close call, but my spirits are lifted, and I know Mr. Ruffs was happy for some playtime.

I'm humming to myself as I try to find my way back to the suite. Not remotely suspecting the ambush that is waiting for me. Or the person who will be behind it.

scene 4

I've heard of blind dates and double dates . . . but ambush dates? My sister has invented a new and horrible category in the world of social interaction. Mere *minutes* ago, she let me know that she had set me up with a boy I've never met. Eva found out that Alex Banks, one of Ivan Banks's sons, is visiting the set—and is in my year in school. *Presto-change-o,* he and I got hooked up for a quick date.

"Eva—you know I can't suddenly *meet* people. I have to prepare!" A recovering shy-girl trick is writing down potential conversation topics to provide a feeling of security.

"You mean write down a bunch of things to talk about?"

"No, I don't mean that!"

Our argument is interrupted by a knock at the door.

Eva takes a deep breath and grins. "Okay, Jess, time to put on your game face."

I pull a smile.

"Yeesh. The one where we're *winning* the game, please." Eva moves to the door. "And don't worry, Alex is friendly. I wouldn't set you up with anyone who wasn't supereasy to talk to."

Does that mean he's friendly? Or is it code for not good-looking?

"And he's cute." Eva's hand is on the doorknob when she turns back with one last piece of whispered advice. "And don't screw up. The Banks family owns *Two Sisters* and half of Hollywood. The better half."

Thanks, E. That doesn't exactly *lessen* the pressure.

Alex arrives. He is genuinely cute—not much taller than me,

wavy black hair, greenish eyes, big white smile. A good smile—but very quickly I am seeing way too much of it, way too close.

You probably don't know the exact measure of your personal space. But you know if someone is in it.

Alex is a space invader. He's right in my face during our elevator ride and walk through the hotel.

I hardly notice. As he talks, and talks, and talks . . . my thoughts are far away, racing around a track, headed nowhere.

I'm on a date. Am I on a date? Did I ever go on a real date with Jeremy? Am I a girl who's dated two boys? Alex is nice, but he's not for me. Not like Jeremy. Don't think about Jeremy. As soon as someone says don't think about something, that's the thing you have to think about. Like Jeremy? Exactly like Jeremy.

Alex looks at me expectantly. "Don't you think?" he asks.

"Well, I'm not sure . . ." . . . what we're talking about.

"You are such an amazing listener, Jessica. Most girls hear the last name Banks, and they start slipping me resumes and head shots. You know, because my dad is so important."

"Mmm-hmm."

"So let's try it!" He pushes open a door onto the beach. A walk on the beach? It's a cloudy day for it. "I've always wanted to go parasailing! I'm so glad you're up for it. Get it? *Up* for it?"

Parasailing? As in, a rider strapped to a parachute and pulled high over the water by a speedboat?

That's what I agreed to?

OMG—dating *is* as dangerous as Abuela said!

We approach a sailboat with the words TANDEM PARASAIL painted on the side. A crowd is waiting.

"Oh, too bad. There's a line. Maybe another time."

"Don't worry about the line, Jessica. The boat is waiting for us."

Eyes eat into us as we cut to the front. Wealthy equals no waiting. But sometimes it equals no popularity, too.

"Let's go, guys!" Alex steps up to the parasailors. "Alex Banks here."

Then I hear two words that you have to hate on any date: Safety. Harness.

The parasailors quickly strap me into a life jacket and harness. Too quickly. "There was a line," I say feebly, looking back.

Sailor smiles. "*Todo es bueno.*"

Alex is strapped beside me. "Are you afraid of heights?" he yells over the roar of the speedboat powering up.

"A little bit." Thanks for asking. Now.

"Great! Me either!"

The boat begins to move. I open my eyes wide. The sand is moving beneath my feet. Then it . . . isn't.

My stomach lurches.

And I'm airborne.

And it's amazing.

I'm a human kite! With an extraordinary view of the ocean crashing against the long white beach below.

I look over to see if Alex is feeling the same rush. He is leaning over with his head buried in his arms. "Alex? Alex?"

No response.

"You all right?"

We're airborne for about ten minutes of graceful floating and swooping, and Alex's head doesn't leave the cradle of his arms for even one of them.

The boat slows and I'm gently deposited back on land with the help of two "catchers." *"Gracias, señores."*

Alex lands on the beach beside me. "Whoa. That was intense."

Maybe he saw more than I thought. We get unstrapped. "Thanks for the sail, Alex. I had fun."

Alex pushes fractionally closer into my space. "I'll tell my dad!" For a guy who doesn't want to be judged by his last name, he can't seem to form a sentence without the words "my dad" in it.

A few drops of rain begin to fall. "I should get back. Eva needs me to run lines with her."

"Well, I wouldn't be much of a *caballero* if I didn't walk you back to your room."

"Oh. Thanks." Chivalry is not dead in Mexico. Unfortunately.

We join the other people heading out of the rain. "Rain?" says one disbelieving tourist. "That wasn't in the brochure."

We walk back through the hotel, Alex pressed to my side with every step, and nonstop talking about our "thrill ride." When we reach the door to my suite, his face is inexplicably close to mine. His green eyes are slashed with gray.

I'm going to turn my cheek toward him if he goes in for a kiss . . . but then . . . for a split second I think: Maybe if he kisses me, I'll start to like him? Maybe there will be . . . zing? I'm still kind of zinging from the parasail. . . .

Alex senses the moment . . . and I let him kiss me, hoping his kisses are better than Jeremy's.

My hopes are quickly dashed.

Or should I say drenched?

Where? Where is all that moisture coming from? And why is it adorable when Petunia slops up my cheek, but gross when Alex does?

I try to move my face away from his, but that causes him to apply . . . *oh no* . . . suction.

I think of Mom's vacuum wrestling with our curtains. During a downpour.

I don't remember thinking all these crazy thoughts when Jeremy kissed me.

Stop it, brain! Stop thinking about Jeremy.

My "stop thinking about Jeremy" command doesn't quite work. When I peel Alex off my face, I am definitely still thinking about Jeremy.

Probably because Jeremy is standing in the hallway, staring at me.

"Heathcliff?" he says in a startled voice.

This looks like a good moment to . . . run and hide. I slip through the door, closing it behind me.

Click!

scene 5

*M*om is the original rhyme-maker in our family. Here's a sample of the health-friendly reminders that E and I used to find tucked into our lunch boxes.

Finish your apple
Crispy and tart
Good for your energy!
Good for your heart!

Un beso,
Mom

I guess the times have changed. Check out what is folded in our handbags as E and I sit beside Mom in church this Sunday morning:

Those teen athletes
Who best live with fame—
Are they the ones
Taking gold from the game?

No. It's athletes with views
Outside the bubble
Who succeed in the world—

And can tell peace from trouble.

Un beso,

Mom

The Mass is all in Spanish, but the order is the same as at home (and, I guess, at Roman Catholic churches all over the world), so it's easy enough to follow. The only new addition to the service is the part at the end where everyone crowds around the TV teen and asks for autographs and photos. Would that be the same all over the world too?

An instant message pops up on E's phone from Keiko: "Brilliant PR going to church, Eva! Way to 'convert' the local press!"

Yeeps. I hit Delete. What is it about that message that goes against my religion?

There is bad news waiting for us back at the hotel. Cast and crew are gathered for an emergency meeting in one of the ballrooms.

Roman takes the podium. He looks like he's been taking longer pulls from his usual High-Stress Slurpee. "I have some unfortunate news. Our Very Special Guest Star is missing."

Creep-creep-peek.

I can practically *feel* eyes wandering in my direction.

No.

No way.

No how.

This cannot have anything to do with me. I didn't even know the Mexico shoot was planning to feature a Very Special Guest Star!

Roman continues: "That's right, Mr. Ruffs is gone."

Oh.

That Very Special Guest Star.

What happened? Did Tommy lose him? Did Mr. Ruffs run off? It's too stolen-from-a-*Two-Sisters*-plotline for Mr. Ruffs to have been petnapped. Isn't it?

"We don't believe that he escaped on his own." Roman looks questioningly at Tommy.

The Pet-Man's face is flushed and angry. "Of course not. I would never be so irresponsible."

OMG—would I?

Be so irresponsible?

Worry haunts me: In my rush to leave Mr. Ruffs's room, did I leave his cage door open? And then the sliding door behind me?

No, I'm sure I closed the cage and the door.

Positive.

Practically, almost 100 percent positive.

And, anyway, Tommy was coming right into the room when I was leaving. Wasn't he?

"We have one piece of good luck. And that is Carlton Winthrop. Quick Carlton heard about our missing performer, and had an immediate brainstorm for a replacement scene. Jeremy? Paige? We'll get you fresh pages ASAP."

The time Eva (and Lavender?) is spending with Carlton doesn't seem to be adding up to more on-screen time.

"Jeremy? Paige?"

Everyone looks around, but I can tell you: Jeremy isn't in the room. I know. I haven't been able to remove my J-dar. The ESP that tells me when Jeremy is near. And he's not. So neither is Paige.

The sinking feeling in my belly can only get . . .

. . . worse.

. . . way worse.

I look at my wrist. Where's my Jessica bracelet? I don't remember putting it on this morning. The last time I saw it was with Mr. Ruffs!

The bracelet might be sitting on the bottom of his cage. Instead of spelling J-E-S-S-I-C-A, it's announcing C-L-U-E.

I've got to get out of here.

The thing about zing?

It can stop you in your tracks, even if you're hot on the trail of a set saboteur and possible puppynapper.

I wasn't looking for zing, but I find it. Right at the golden diving pond in the lobby.

Poetry, country songs, and ruins of a once-great civilization—they are all going to have to take a backseat in the best-for-broken-hearts sweepstakes. I've made a new discovery: mariachi.

The band is made up of a violin, a trumpet, three sizes of guitars, and the singer. Some of the heat of the day has found its way into the music—bitter with sweet, and *passionate.* If I could understand it, I'd speak perfect Mexican.

The only word I understand is *amor,* but a friendly bellhop catches my eye, and explains as the music sears the air. The singer was a revolutionary, condemned to death. He was going to die with dignity, asking that he be buried in his traditional shawl instead of a coffin, with his cartridge belts arranged to form a cross. And they could write these final words over his tomb—with a thousand bullets!

Do we know how to suffer or what?

126

What can I say? Mexicans have zing.

Beside me, I notice another guest caught by the music—Madame Muu, the tall *turista*. Still dressed like a cartoon of a cliché in the same exact outfit, including the enormous glasses and hat.

When the music ends, she unfolds her hands, clapping. Then I see . . . sun! Ten perfect little suns, one painted on each fingernail.

In that instant, I know who's hiding under the masses of muumuu. And why.

*E*verything falls into place.

After all, I have an instinct for these things. And when I catch this set-wrecker, I hope they throw the book at her, or at least the *page*.

I go straight to Eva and Mom with the whole story.

The clincher is the motivation: Who benefits from the stolen scripts? Look no further than the person who scores juicy new scenes with every rewrite.

I bust in on Mom clicking away on her Sidekick. E is opening a big blue envelope. "Look at this. An invitation to a surprise party."

"Like we need more surprises around here," says Mom.

I take a quick look at the invite. The party will be on the same floor where I saw the tacky tourist exit the elevator.

"Everyone thinks Al is throwing it. You know how he thinks every episode should end in a party? The lines of reality and writing are getting very blurry with him."

"E, he's not the only one."

I tell my sister everything I suspect, finishing by naming Paige as the tourist-in-disguise! And why a disguise? Because she's the saboteur! Partway through, Mom puts down her Sidekick. She and E exchange an unreadable glance.

Then . . . cheering, high fives, congratulations? Not even close.

Mom frowns. "Jessica, can you see how this could sound like an excuse to spy on Paige and Jeremy?"

I immediately give her my Huffy-Puffy Face.

Ay! I mean, my Fierce Face for Fear and Trembling.

Mom holds up her arms. "Okay, okay, Paige is not the most . . ." She stops. She takes my hand. "Jess, Paige is not a part of this. You have nothing tying her to any of the incidents. And lots of women wear nail polish."

"With little gold suns painted on?"

"As for motivation," Mom continues, "it was an awful lot of work to go through on the chance that she'd get a bigger role in the show."

"All the more reason to pursue Paige! She's great at hiding her tracks. No one else would suspect her but me."

"Well, that's true." At least Eva sees things my way. Or that is what I think until she calls Roman and says words I thought would never leave her lips: "Can you please tell them to hold up filming for a minute? I'm going to be late."

Eva clicks off her cell.

"E? What's wrong?" My sister never causes delays on her projects. She had her doctor reschedule her appendectomy until after the end of shooting last year. (That extra wince of pain in the "Farewell, Fluffy" episode wasn't all for the tree kangaroo.)

"Tell me that you won't follow Paige around."

My temper flies up like a kite. "Why are you defending her, E? Now you're on her side, too?"

"You're the one I'm looking out for, Jess." Usually when I get mad, E gets mad right back, but not this time. "Paige wasn't involved with this. If you'd asked me, I would have told you that she was shooting her scene with Jeremy when the prop presents were stolen." Eva looks sad and worried. "I know you're upset about . . . Please, tell me that you'll leave Paige alone. Promise me."

I don't say anything.

The thrill of believing . . . well, hoping . . . that Paige was the thief deflates into a sour lump in my belly. "Did you see Murphy at the shoot too?"

"Huh? Yeah, I think he was there, talking to Lighting Guy Bob."

Then I'm all out of suspects.

I can't look at Eva or Mom. I've never felt more like a Sad Hoper.

Paige isn't the props thief.

That's not what she stole at all.

scene 7

Think too much about the person you're trying to avoid . . . and abracadabra! He appears.

"Hi, Jessica." Jeremy is walking to his suite at the exact moment I'm exiting Eva's. He waves a small package at me in greeting. "Bad news about Mr. Ruffs, huh?"

You have no idea. I nod.

"I could help?" Jeremy suggests. "If you were trying to figure things out?"

In the glorious days now known as the Pre-Paige Period, Jeremy and I had been a great team, working together to catch the Secret Admirer. "I don't think so."

"Oh." Jeremy doesn't say anything, just fiddles with the package. Then he says, "Hey, we can be friends, right?"

I dare a glance up at him. He's serious.

"Yeah. I guess." If your friend is someone you want to kiss with full zing, while simultaneously tearing the fake eyelashes off anyone who'd want to kiss him. That's friendly, right?

He smiles. "Then come help me through this. I'll need a friend." He takes a DVD out of the package: *Horror High*. Jeremy had a small role in the film. "I never saw it in the theaters. And neither did anyone else. I've got my laptop set up on the terrace." I remember that Jeremy had actually been optimistic about the movie when he was making it, but the reviews were awful. His role was edited down to shots of him babbling the usual scary movie speeches: "Everyone who goes into the attic has been disappearing. So let's go to the attic . . . *aaaaaah!*"

And speaking of foolish decisions that can lead only to certain disaster . . . I say: "Okay."

There is only one reason I agree to go with Jeremy through his suite and onto the beachfront patio: because I want to.

There's not much that says "Jeremy" about his suite. It's outrageously luxe, like Eva's. There is a crayon drawing, probably by his little brother, Jack, a couple of *Space Frontier* graphic novels, and a big binder from his favorite charity, Heifer.org. No Paige-tracks anywhere.

We sit outside and he sets up the movie. We watch the screen in silence, carefully sitting beside each other without touching elbows. At least, I'm carefully sitting. Jeremy might be regularly sitting.

Now, you may not have seen Jeremy's bad movie, but you've seen one like it: Everyone sounds like they're yelling, the camera is bobbing like a bumblebee, and the music hits two notes, screech and screechier. From the corner of my eye, I can see embarrassment heating Jeremy's face.

"No wonder the reviewers called it *Horrible High*." He tries to laugh it off.

Without a word, I press some buttons on the laptop, and flip over to Language Selection. I choose French with English sub-titles.

The mood of the film is instantly different.

"Wow," Jeremy says after a few minutes of watching himself speak quick, urgent French. "How'd you think of that?"

You want the truth? E and I watched *Waterworld* one time and couldn't turn off the French with subtitles. Everything that had seemed overly dramatic in English came across as weighty and important in French. And movies with subtitles? They're for people who'd rather be reading a book, so even when the movie is awful, there's a feeling that it's awful because it's *too intellectual.*

I don't want to tell Jeremy about *Waterworld*—there's no kind way to compare his movie to one of Hollywood's biggest disasters. So I say, "Your film had a French feel to it."

Jeremy moves surprisingly fast, and has his arms around me in a huge hug. "Thanks, Jess," he says into my hair.

I'm suddenly . . . what's the name of that feeling again?

Oh, yes, I remember . . . happy. Happy settles on me as soft as snow.

I hug him back and breathe in . . . cigarettes and overpriced perfume.

"What?" he asks as I pull away.

I don't say anything for a long moment. Then: "Nothing. I was reminded of your new habit, that's all."

"Which is?"

"Secondhand smoking."

All the shiny is off the moment.

I leave without saying goodbye.

*A*nd third-rate actresses!

Could we please hit Rewind and Replay?

I say: "I was reminded of your new habit, that's all."

Jeremy says: "Which is?"

And I say: "Secondhand smoking . . . and third-rate actresses!"

Wouldn't it have been so cool if I had thought to say that then?

Instead of, you know, just now.

scene 8

*T*ime to focus on Project Stop Skunk. Or should it be re-named Project Stop Sabotage?

If I can get back into Mr. Ruffs's room, I might be able to find some evidence of what happened to him. (Or at least find my incriminatingly chewed bracelet!)

But first I have to find the room.

I'm not sure which end of the hotel map is up when I see a familiar cornrowed head. Murphy is bent over his laptop, pounding on the keys. He is sitting in an isolated corner of an empty lounge, mostly hidden behind some flowering bushes.

I approach and peek over his shoulder. Is he working on lyrics for a new Runny Snots song?

"Hi, Murphy."

The guy jumps out of his seat, in a jittery imitation of Anxious Al. He snaps his laptop shut. "Jessica. Whaddaya doing here?"

I shrug. "I'm trying to find out where 'here' is."

The worry lines ease off Murphy's face. "Gimme the map. I'll show you. Whaddaya looking for?"

"*Celebración* Suites."

Murphy shows me on the map. "Left at the elevators. Right at the giant picture of Mr. Banks. Then follow Fiesta Suites until they turn into *Celebración*."

I must look confused, because Murphy puts his laptop into a messenger bag and volunteers to get me going in the right direction.

"I haven't been down that way. Who you visiting?"

"Mr. Ruffs. Well, his room anyway."

"Clue catching?" Murphy must know my reputation.

"Trying to."

I see one of the housekeepers in her green and gold Hotel Banks uniform. I duck behind Murphy as we pass.

Another housekeeper approaches. I hold up my hand awkwardly in front of my face until she passes. Darting a quick sideways look, I can see she's not Rita.

Murphy stops. "Jumpy, aren't you?" He's looking at me suspiciously. "Something you want to tell me?"

"No. It's nothing. I'm innocent!" *Yeesh.* "I'm innocent"—are they the two guiltiest-sounding words in the world? Or is it just the way I say them?

Murphy looks unconvinced. Will he tell Roman that I was looking for Mr. Ruffs's room and acting suspicious? I blurt out: "There is a housekeeper who let me in to visit with Mr. Ruffs before he went missing." Murphy's eyebrows rise high. "I was playing with him. I was—*he* was lonely. That's all. But it's better if I don't see Rita again now." I grip Murphy's arm. "Please. You have to believe me."

"Okay, Jessica. I believe you." Someone sees me as I really am? "No sister of Eva's would be the dognapping type."

Whew! "Thanks, Murphy. You can see why I want to find Mr. Ruffs."

"Sure." Murphy has managed to lead us to the *Celebración* Suites part of the hotel. I'm trying to remember which room was

Mr. Ruffs's when Murphy goes up to 309 and knocks. Murphy must have heard familiar voices inside the room.

The door opens to reveal someone I really want to see.

And someone I really don't.

*R*uff! *Ruff!*

"Mr. Ruffs! You're back!" I bend down to give the cuddly cocker spaniel a huge hug. The better to ignore the people in the room: Murphy, Tommy, and . . . Jeremy.

Tommy's face is filled with joy and relief. "I owe it all to Jeremy. He just found Mister and brought him home."

Murphy bends to pet Mr. Ruffs. "How'd you do it, Jer?"

"I was looking for someone, and I found myself in this private courtyard, and there was Mr. Ruffs. It looks like the hotel staff was caring for him. There was a bowl of dog food left out, and some chew toys."

"Any idea how he wound up there?" Tommy asks anxiously.

Jeremy looks right at me when he answers. "No. Nothing."

In my bones, I know Jeremy is lying. But about what?

*A*s any actor will tell you, the audience reacts more to the person delivering the lines than they do to the actual words. You know it's true. "You are in so much trouble!" shouted by your sister post-chewed-Jimmy Choos (Petunia is the best dog in the world, but she's not *perfect*) is a lot different from "You are in so much trouble!" shouted by an angry mob storming the local prison. (Yes, I'm two-thirds of the way through *To Kill a Mockingbird*.)

And the words "I had a great time with you—let's go out again" mean something different coming from Alex now than they would've from Jeremy Jones a week ago. But it's a fair guess that I'd be bumbling my reply no matter who was on the other end of the phone line.

"Um . . . go out?"

Alex laughs. "Yeah, it's like staying inside by yourself, only the opposite."

He is nice. I could like him as a friend. I just don't want to go splashing around in his kisses again.

"Oh, yes, out. Gotcha." Obviously my IQ points tumble in times of high stress.

"Uh, it's just that I'm busy . . . looking into the sabotage on the set, so . . . I don't really have time. . . ."

"That stuff? I'll tell you about it."

"You will?" The skunking, the inking, the petnapping—what could Alex know about any of it?

"Sure! So I'll meet you in the lobby at three o'clock. Roman is going to drive us."

A date with a guy I don't *like* like, joined by another guy who can't stand me. And here I thought getting my heart stomped via national television was as low as my social life could go.

I get to the lobby a few minutes before three and see Roman waiting. He does something surprising when he sees me: he smiles.

I realize that Roman has teeth. I mean, I suspected he had teeth, but since he never, *ever* smiled while I was around, I lacked visual confirmation.

Roman pats the seat next to him for me to sit down. "I don't know what's keeping Alex, he's never late," he says, checking his watch.

I'd like to say something back, but all I'm thinking is: Roman has teeth. That's not exactly the kind of thing I should blurt out in conversation—though I usually do.

Roman leans in closer. "Look, Jessica, Alex's dad—my boss, the *big* boss—is thrilled to see his son so happy. I guess Alex had a tough year—found out that his last girlfriend was a big cheat and all-around liar. He hasn't been happy since, well, now. Meeting you."

Whoa. I don't want to make Alex unhappy, but I don't want to be the cause of happy, either.

"I know why you're so quiet." Roman looks away. "It's the petition, isn't it? I shouldn't have started that to gather support for banning you. But you can imagine that the difficulties with the Very Special Guest Stars made my job tough."

Petition?

"And, I have to admit that dozens of those people probably would not have signed had I not been so stern with them. And, of course, I'm not proud of those posters."

Posters? There had been some "Ban the Jinx" posters on the set, but Eva told me they were about someone named Jinx Jinkins in the accounting department.

Wait a minute . . . Jinx Jinkins? Could that name *be* any more made up?

"But still, you were just a girl who hit a bad-luck patch there with Kutcher, Clooney, and the Olsens, and . . ." Roman's face starts clouding over. "Anyway, I feel bad about all that—especially the limerick." He laughs. "But it's not my fault that you-know-what rhymes with your nickname!"

My mind is buzzing: Jess, Bess, Cess, Dess . . .

Through with his soul-cleansing confession, Roman holds out his hand. "Let's start fresh. No golf carts. No marmalade. No jinx. No history."

I summon up a shaky smile, gripping his hand weakly. "No problem."

Ess, Fess, Guess . . . uh-oh. What if my nickname is not Jess? Yikes, brain, do not go there.

I never thought the moment would come when Roman turned down the scare-glare enough for me to ask: "You weren't angry enough to send me a . . . skunk?"

"Skunk?" Roman looks genuinely puzzled. "What do you mean?"

"Or are you missing any mailing labels from your office?"

Roman shrugs. "Who knows? If people are stealing empty boxes, I guess mailing labels might get taken too."

It hadn't made much sense for Roman to be behind the skunking— the man is obsessed with *positive* publicity for his show. (And any skunk he would send would definitely be addressed to me, not E.) But it still feels good to read the truth in his for-once-not-narrowed eyes.

I see Alex walking toward us. The expression on his face surprises me. He's thin-lipped and angry, *not* happy to see me. "I don't like being played, Jessica."

"What?"

"If you're into somebody else, you should say it."

"B-but I . . ." I didn't want to hurt his feelings. I have no idea what's the right thing to say now. He looks so angry, so hurt. "I—I'm sorry, Alex."

"So it *is* true." Alex looks disgusted. And no way am I brave enough to look at Roman. "I was completely wrong about you. I never thought you'd be the type to come on to one guy while you were into someone else."

Um . . . *come on to*?

"And I had to hear it from someone else, instead of you? Man, I feel like a jerk." Alex nods at Roman. "Let's go."

Roman glares at me. Our new start just got a new ending.

"Jessica . . ." Alex looks at me, trying to decide what to say. "Forget it. Goodbye. I don't want to see you again."

This has to stop: guys I'm not even dating are dumping me!

Alex turns away, but then looks back toward me. Is he going to explain what he knows about the set sabotage? He frowns. "Jessica, if you knew anything about being a friend, you would have been honest . . . and told me about Heathcliff."

Heathcliff? Where did he hear that name?

Oh.

Freaking.

No.

"**E**va, this is all your fault!"

Someone to dump a date's worth of frustration on—that's what big sisters are for, right?

E had been reading a script on the couch, but she gets up to face me. "Calm down, Jessica. What happened?"

"Look, any *normal* sister would have made me some CD of 'Songs for Getting Over Boys' or something—but no, you have to go all superstar on me with some slobbery insta-date."

"Hey! Alex is a good dresser."

"Slob*bery*. Not slob."

"Oh. You mean . . . *ewwww*." But does she apologize? No, she keeps on being Eva Ortiz. "Well, if you wanted a CD, then you could have asked for it. And if you don't want some guy slobbering on you, then speak up about that, too."

I glare. She shrugs. "Do you want to talk about it?" I don't say a word. "Thought so." Eva picks up a package that lies on the coffee table. "This came for you."

She throws it to me. Not rough, but not gently, either.

This package is a small rectangular box wrapped in brown paper, addressed to me.

You better believe I'm checking for airholes.

It doesn't rattle when shaken. No scratching sounds either. I give it a quick sniff.

"Open it already," says Eva. She says this from across the room.

Slowly, I peel off the paper, revealing a simple cardboard box.

Slowly, I lift one corner of the lid.

Slowly, I lift another corner. Then the whole lid.

Slowly, I try to figure out what I'm looking at.

Eva steps closer. "Looks like chewed-up bits of that bracelet of yours." I shake the box. There is nothing else in it. No note. "Why would someone send that to you, Jessica?"

I wish I knew.

Act
IV

"I believe in fate. I believe that everything happens for a reason, but I think it's important to seek out that reason—that's how you learn."

—DREW BARRYMORE

*I*t's time for another surprise.

Surprise party, that is. The cast and some of the crew from *Two Sisters* huddle in a large dimly lit suite.

Eva, Mom, and I arrive together. No one seems to know the story behind the mystery invitations.

I approach the man most people think is our host. "Hello, Al."

"Hi, kid." He offers me a beverage. "Red Bull?"

"No, thanks." I hear those things give you hummingbird heart, but Anxious Al is guzzling like a Stretchcalade at the gas pump.

"What's the party all about, Al?"

"Huh? Everybody's asking me that. I don't know. I do NOT know. This is me"—he points to his face—"this is what I look like in a state of not knowing!"

Whoa. Step away from the ultracaffeinated beverages.

I feel bad for revving up Al's anxiety level. In my most soothing voice: "It seems like the writing team has been responding well to the pressure of all the quick changes."

Al shrugs. "The only good news lately is the Paige-Jeremy romance; we're planning a fantastic story line for them."

Woo-freaking-hoo.

Followed by: *wooo wooo!* That's right: my J-dar goes off.

"Hi, Jessica." Jeremy arrives at my side. He's dressed in a black polo and tan shorts. He looks over his shoulder before he asks me in a low voice, "Did you get my . . . message?"

"Message? You mean the one you sent through Alex?"

The line in Jeremy's jaw tightens. He *was* the one who told Alex! I knew it! Jeremy doesn't apologize. "Why shouldn't Alex know about Heathcliff?"

Ouch. Is it me, or does the name Heathcliff sound more fake every time it's said out loud?

I'm flustered and angry. "Heathcliff isn't real . . . ly . . . he isn't really any of your business."

A suspicious light gleams in Jeremy's eye. "What are you saying?"

I don't answer. I can't. I stare at my feet.

That's what I'm doing when the lights flick off.

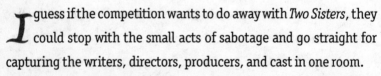

I guess if the competition wants to do away with *Two Sisters*, they could stop with the small acts of sabotage and go straight for capturing the writers, directors, producers, and cast in one room.

Or am I the only person paranoid enough to think that?

Then again: maybe I'm not paranoid enough.

Possibly it's because Murphy mentioned that the ghost of Marilyn Monroe appears at the Roosevelt, but when an eerie, little-girlish voice fills the room with a warbly "Happy Birthday," all I can think is: Marilyn?

"H-h-happy b-i-i-rthday to youuu . . ."

A huge cake appears, candles burning on top. And in the flickering light, I recognize the sunset-painted fingertips holding up the platter.

The same polish as Paige's.

The same polish as her copycat mama's.

Roman finds the lights, which he brings up to full brightness. We all watch Paige's mom approach her daughter with the cake, still singing away. A tuft of white hair over large, anxious eyes pokes out of the bulky bag on Paige's shoulder. Tink takes one look at Mama Paige and ducks back into the bag. Smart dog.

The room is decorated with a huge selection of brightly wrapped presents and strings of colored lights. The presents are so professionally perfect, they could almost be the ones that were stolen from the props tent.

No.

She.

Didn't.

OMG—she did! Paige's *mother* was the tall and tacky tourist! All this time, I had been thinking the outfit was too outrageous to be real—and it was! Mama Paige was wearing a disguise to get close to Paige. And to steal decorations for the party.

Muumuu-free, Mama Paige is sporting a fake-bake; bottle-blond hair; mile-high clear plastic heels; and a way-too-short-for-her-age skirt with matching tutu. I recognize the skirt as an imitation of Paige's Golden Globes outfit.

The birthday song ends, and Mama Paige lets out a giggle. "Welcome, everyone! Hope you don't mind me 'borrowing' some decorations! But we all know nothing is too good for Paige!"

I'm standing next to Amber, who tells Roman, "I can't believe it. It's the mother!"

Roman growls. "Do you think she'll go weepily bitter on us again?"

"No, she's playing psychotically perky today. I thought you got rid of her?"

"I did. She got around me somehow." Roman's voice is flat and angry. "She is one tough *cucaracha*."

"Hello, Mom." Paige looks startled, worried, and hopeful.

That's when it hits me: no matter how weird and manipulative this woman is, she keeps on being Paige's mom. *Forever!*

Paige looks over at the pile of presents. "You got all these for me?"

Her mother's toothy grin doesn't dim. "Not exactly, baby! They're decorations. This party is your gift!"

"This party" is a room full of Paige's embarrassed coworkers and a big cake with burning candles dripping into the frosting.

Paige opens a box. Empty. Of course. I'd like Mama Paige better if she stole real presents for her daughter, instead of a shiny back-drop for herself. Is the party a straight-up audition for the *Two Sisters* team, and nothing to do with Paige?

"Mom?" Paige shakes another box. She doesn't seem to realize that her mom ripped off the props tent to fill the room with sparkly, empty packages. If I was her, I wouldn't want to realize it either.

Has her mother bought Paige anything? Mama Paige looks like she is trying to find cue cards to read. Behind me, Roman grunts: "Tabloid train wreck." Paige is about to burst out crying.

Everyone is watching the Paige-and-Mama drama. Everyone but me. I'm watching Jeremy.

Why?

Because I can.

He reaches into his pocket. Then his hand plunges into the pile of fake presents. His fingers pull back, wrapped around a small blue box. Tiffany blue.

"Linda? I think Paige's present fell behind the . . . decorations."

Mama Paige's hand tears toward the box. Her fingers roll hungrily over the satiny ribbon. By force of will—and the eyes watching—Mama Paige slaps the box into Paige's hand. "For my baby girl!" she says triumphantly.

Paige gives a small, childlike smile. She undoes the ribbon, and pulls open the velvet box. Inside are a typed note and a silver bracelet with a kite charm dangling from it.

Paige reads the note aloud: "'A kite floats/At the place in the sky/Where it floated yesterday. Yosa Buson.'" She turns to her momster. "Who's Yosa?"

Her mom looks blank for a moment. The uneasy silence must stretch only a few seconds, but it feels longer. Then Mama Paige pops out with: "Yosa is the newest jewelry collection at Tiffany's!"

"A signature line?"

"You bet!"

"Is this kite about . . . the time I asked for a kite, and you said, 'No way'?"

"Sure!"

"Oh, Mama!" Paige plunges toward her mother. Her mom squeezes her back. You can practically hear bones clacking.

"We should check the presents for hidden cameras," whispers Amber. Roman smirks. Then looks worried.

Mama Paige cries out, "It's all so *Pretty Woman*!"

"I want the fairy tale!" answers Paige, in her best Julia Roberts.

"I want the airsick bags," mutters Amber.

Murphy is the first to leave, pulling Lavender with him. "I've had a great time," he mutters, "but this wasn't it."

I hear Roman take a cell phone call. "What?" he barks. "Are you sure? Well, you know what to do."

Roman lets out a low, bitter curse. This time it must be about Mama Paige.

It can't be about me.

Absolutely not me this time.

"What is it, boss?" asks Amber.

"These rent-a-cops better not screw this up. We have someone who can ID the petnapper. A housekeeper let someone into the room."

My reaction? In a word: *gulp*.

The cast loves shooting at the beach—anything to make the moment more authentic. I love shooting at the beach—anything to keep me away from petnapper-identifying housekeepers.

Jeremy is talking with Lighting Guy Bob about the technical aspects of working with natural light. Lavender and Murphy are running lines—though it looks like it's for some fight scene that I don't remember in the script. Paige's mom is sitting on a beach chair labeled HOT MAMA, yelling into her cell phone. My mom is rehearsing with Eva, prepping E for the emotional reunion in the "Finding Mr. Ruffs" scene.

```
Girls at the beach in Mexico
in colorful tankinis. They
approach a small furry animal
trundling across the sand.


                  EVA
Those bright eyes . . . that
```

154

```
brown   hair  .  .  .  could   it
be  .  .  .
```

```
           LAVENDER
Mr. Ruffs! Is it you?


            PAIGE
Can someone lotion my back?
```

And me?

I'm returning a scrappy, pink mass of aspiring dog to his owner.

"Jessica, are you done Tinkling?"

Ugh. Paige giggles with every Tinkle. The poor little beastie was already about the ugliest creature on the planet—clinging to entry in the dog family by his manicured fingernails—and Paige had to go and hang a joke name on him. A seriously unfunny joke name.

"He liked his walk, Paige."

I'm returning Tink to Paige's bag. I had heard the little guy whining away. When I took a peek in the bag, Tink was struggling under the weight of his ill-fitting Coach collar, and I could tell he needed a walk. Poor little mutt. (Oops, he's definitely a purebred; Paige wouldn't buy anything without a label.)

I was able to get Tink out of his bag, but I couldn't get him out of his pink cashmere Juicy hoodie. Paige insists he loves it, and, well . . . guess what Paige is wearing over her bathing suit? As if the gak factor wasn't at an all-time high with matching dog-and-dork outfits, Paige is also sporting an iPod encased in a matching microhoodie as well. What's next—teeny fuzzy tops for her pens, lipsticks, paper clips?

I smooch poor old Tink goodbye—he'll take a nice nap now—and head over to the spread that Craft Services has laid out.

I help myself to some of the ice cream that's melting in the sun—you know the starlets aren't going to hit it.

Paige wanders over with her water jug. "Jessica, you should know that ice cream has more fat per ounce than actual fat."

Talking to Paige, even my hair starts to hurt.

Paige looks closer at my ice cream choice. "So Beyoncé," she says with a knowing little smile.

"Huh?"

"Butter pecan? B's *favorite* flavor." Paige is looking at me like this information is more common than the name of the president. "Some people see a trend and *have* to follow."

Grr! This from the girl who'd wear a diaper if it said Dior on it.

Jeremy must notice the strangled look on my face because he comes right over. He hands Paige a tiny pink hoodie. "Your cell was ringing."

Paige whips open her phone. "It's a message from your mom, Remy. She is such a sweetheart." She is? I never met her. "Look at my cell phone. It has our picture on it."

"Yours and mine?" asks Jeremy.

"No, silly," says Paige, showing him the screen on the phone. "Mine and your mom's. And look at this text message. Check out all the Xs and Os. I am totally *in* with your mom."

"And my agent."

"I thought your mom was your agent."

"She is."

Paige looks confused for a moment. "Oh, that's funny. I love a funny guy."

Fortunately my own cell phone distracts me. My new signature ring is the latest from Spilt Sugar. Do you know it?

I hate everything I loved about you—
The things you did, the things you do.

Your crazy smile, your crazy kiss.
I got a list of what I don't miss!

I chose the song strictly because of its rockin' beat.

I pick up my phone. "Hello? Hello?" No one is on the line.

Then I see Jeremy with *his* phone out. "Hello?"

What? We had reprogrammed our phones with the same song!

This is horrible. This is terrible. This is . . . the sound of *my* phone ringing now. And of course, I'm so freaked out that I'm fumbling with the phone, while Spilt Sugar sings:

I have a life that's better now.
Who needs your hassle anyhow?
The way you dance, the way you shout,
I've got a list to never think about!

Jeremy and I catch eyes, and then look away from each other as we talk on our phones. "I'm fine, Abuela. . . . How's your hip

feeling? . . . How's my Petunia? . . . No, no rain. . . . No, no boys. . . .
Yes, please, put Dad on."

Yes, my heart is still broken.

After checking in with Dad and suffering through his Mexican
weather forecast (*Chile today! Hot tamale!*), I bring the phone
over to Mom so that she can say hello. "Mom, can I borrow your
Sidekick?"

"Sure."

"Dad's on my cell. You're the best."

"Yes, so you've told me . . . repeatedly . . . since the birthday
party. Give yourself a ten for excellent judgment." She takes the
phone. "Hi, Rob."

I should leave it alone.

Drop it.

Let it go.

But I can't.

I take the Sidekick from Mom's purse, and Google *Yosa Buson
Tiffany and Co.*

Nothing comes up.

Then I try *Yosa Buson.* He's not a Tiffany designer; he
was an eighteenth-century Haiku poet. I think of the silly haiku

that Jeremy had written for me about Petunia: "Stubby-tailed doggie/Opposite of L.A.'s hype—/Happy and so fat."

The facts point to one conclusion: Paige's mother never bought her that bracelet. Jeremy bought it and passed it off as a gift from Mama Paige to save her feelings. But had Jeremy meant the bracelet for Paige—or for me?

If he meant it for me, then what did the poem mean? The kite is floating in the same place? What kite?

Or am I fooling myself—turning into a Sad Hoper—like when I tried to convince E and Mom (and myself) that Paige was the saboteur? Maybe Jeremy quotes poetry to all girls? Maybe kites have a secret meaning for him and Paige?

"Two minutes, people," calls Roman.

Paige steps right up. "We all have to work together to make this happen." She flings her arms wide, almost whomping off Roman's ear. "We're like a hand—no finger can point on its own."

There is a moment of puzzled silence. Then Paige's mom claps.

Eva rushes over to whisper to me before taking her place. "What were you doing with Paige?"

"Nothing. Just taking her dog for a walk. Why?"

My sister has a strange look on her face. "I had this weird

thought. Like if you hung around Paige, your jinx would kick in."

My mouth drops open in surprise. "I admit I *used to have* a temporary jinx, but how could you think that I'd purposely bring bad luck to Paige?"

And why didn't I ever think of that? Um . . . not that I'm thinking of it now.

Or now.

Not now, either.

There are only a few lines of dialogue to shoot, but Roman demands take after take. He's not satisfied with the scene. Finally, Lighting Guy Bob tells him, "Roman, we've lost the light."

"Okay, okay. That's a wrap." Roman frowns. "It's all right. But we need spectacular. Who can get me spectacular?" For some reason, his eyes fall on the least likely suspect: Anxious Al.

I'm late to the presentation at the writers' room. The hotel is harder to navigate now that I jump behind fire extinguishers every time a housekeeping cart turns the corner.

Our host will be the last to arrive. Amber makes the announcement: "He's on his way."

Anxious Al is coming to address the cast. Or what's left of Al is coming. He was in pretty bad shape when Roman left him with the directive to scrap the rest of the Mexico scenes and bring him something "spectacular." Till further notice, Anxious Al's nickname is being changed to "Shaking and Deathly Pale Al."

The writers are huddled at one end of the room. The actors and their "people" are gathered around the long wooden table. Lavender and Murphy are both on their cells. Mom and Eva are reviewing publicity photos. (I overhear Eva getting an eight in good taste; why isn't this parenting fad over yet?) I'm scribbling notes on some of the small Hotel Banks pads that have been left behind. The better to ignore Jeremy, Paige, and Mama Paige having a cozy chat at the other end of the table. It's a disturbing sight, and not only because Paige and Mama are dressed in matching micro–tank tops sequined with the words: Love Me!

On my notepad I review the new question: What does it mean now that we know Mama Paige was the props thief? Was she responsible for any of the other trouble? The skunking/the inking/the dognapping/the Jessica bracelet package? Mama Paige will do anything to get a few more bites of fame—but it's hard to know what she thinks would help her. Wearing yards of fluorescent pink cotton and stealing empty packages equals an audition for *Two Sisters* producers? That's mental math I can't follow.

Amber claps. *Chop-chop.* "He's walking down the hall!"

The rumor is "major changes" are coming. I hope it's not major changes in Al's mental health.

The handle turns. The door begins to open.

Eva, Mom, and I hold our breath. Paige places a call on her cell. "Mom and I need *designer* tissues. Not Kleenex."

Shaking and Deathly Pale Al enters. Only he isn't shaking and deathly pale anymore. I'm surprised by what I *don't* see: no eye twitch, no jittery limbs, and no copious sweating. He's no more green-cheese-colored than usual, and his shirt does not appear to have been slept in for more than two days. All in all, I'm looking at "Better-than-Average Al."

Everyone in the room breathes a sigh of relief.

Well, almost everyone.

"Are you sure? Nicole Kidman uses Kleenex? Are you positive? I want written or video confirmation on that. None of this 'my cousin's best friend saw her with Kleenex.' "

I look at Al, and relax a little bit . . . a little too soon. His voice is high and excited. "We're moving the show to a top-secret location. Your flight plans are in the enclosed envelopes, but please, for security's sake, don't open them till we get to the airport."

Has Al overdosed on drama? Or Red Bull?

His eye twitch has been replaced by a gleam, a wild gleam.

Man, I never thought I'd miss that twitch.

He sweeps out of the room, while the rest of us stare at the sealed brown envelopes that Amber hands out.

Paige is still jabbering away on her cell. I'm not sure she heard a word Al said. She certainly didn't hear the words "don't open."

Tear. Paige puts down her cell long enough to announce, "London, Wisconsin? Whoa, that city is *so* not where I thought it was."

Wisconsin?

The show is not going there for the sun, so it must be for the "stars."

The writers' room erupts into conversation.

"Wisconsin? What is Al thinking?"

"Does Roman know about this?"

I see Lavender nod toward the door, and her bf follows her out into the hallway. I wait for a few moments, and then I follow Murphy.

The two hurry into a nearby lounge, pulling their chairs behind some potted palms. I stand against the wall around the corner.

"Will you whisper?" Lavender demands.

"I am whispering!" Murphy says loudly.

"Look, everything was all set up here. What are we going to do?"

"Don't worry, Lav. I can arrange it again."

"You sure? It has to look *believable*."

"It's what I do. If you don't trust me, it's not gonna work." He gestures with his arm, making the barbed wire tattoo slash the air.

What? What are they talking about? There's no way it's romantic plans that just got canceled.

More sabotage? Questions are buzzing in my brain.

That's the only reason I get caught.

Otherwise I would have been watching out for her.

"*Hola, niña.*"

"Holy . . . I mean, *hola.*"

It's her. The woman who thinks she can identify me as the pet-napper. Rita the housekeeper.

"*Cómo está tu perro?*" Rita asks.

I walk beside her as she pushes her cart down the hall—I don't want Lavender and Murphy overhearing *me.*

"My dog?" The words race out of my mouth. "Look, Rita, I can explain. Mr. Ruffs isn't exactly my dog, but I wanted to visit him. I shouldn't have lied to you, but I didn't steal him. And now he's back, so maybe we don't have to talk to Roman?"

Rita looks at me blankly.

"I could get you an autograph from my sister," I offer weakly. "And a *Two Sisters* T-shirt."

"Speak. More. Slowly. Please."

"Oh, sorry. *Lo siento. Mi perro no es mi perro.*"

"Ah." Rita doesn't look too surprised to hear that "my dog is not my dog." "My manager asked if any housekeepers knew about a stolen dog."

"Rita, I promise, *yo no robado el perro!* I wouldn't. I couldn't."
Did I just say "I did not robbered the dog?"

"*Calmate, niña. Ay!* You are so like my granddaughter. Thinking
I do not have *ojos y orejas,* eyes and ears. Of course, you would not
hurt a dog."

"You know that? You can tell?"

"*Claro. La verdad padece pero no perece.*" She pushes her cart
into the large steel service elevator. "*Adiós, niña.*"

The elevator doors begin to close. I don't know what to say.
Then I do: "*Gracias. Muchas gracias,* Rita."

I t's a quick *adiós* to the land of sun, sand, and surf. And hello to
the land of the Cheese and Sausage Festival.

Al and the writing staff are giddy with excitement about the new
plot twist: tracking down Mr. Ruffs's twin to a Green Bay Packers
game at Lambeau Field. Says Al: "Sure, we threw around the usual
places—Hawaii, São Paulo, Paris—but aren't they awfully overdone?"

Wisconsin is the new Hawaii! You heard it here first. And possibly last.

"Of course, the best part is that a Very Special Guest Star is lined
up," said Roman.

Discussion over. Locations switched. And overnight, the cast and a skeleton crew are moved from south of the border to south of the other border.

We're checking into the Badger Inn.

I wonder if I'm getting looks because I'm the sister of a TV star. Or is it because I'm Latina? Milk isn't as white as New London, Wisconsin. "Mom, are people staring because I'm Latina?" I ask in a low voice.

"It's the coats," answers the eavesdropping hotel clerk. "Latinos—not unusual. Winter coats at this time of year—unusual." It's first thing in the morning and only sixty degrees out, so of course all of us Angelenos are shivering in our coats. The locals are in T-shirts and shorts. "Plenty of time for wearing coats around here."

I try to sound a little more worldly. "So what's it like to live in the state that makes the most . . . um, milk?"

The clerk looks at me. "That would be California."

It would?

We're next to Paige as we check in. She says, "There must be a lot of bears here, right?" The clerk looks at her blankly. "Is it true they won't attack if you carry a flashlight?"

"Depends how fast you carry it," he answers.

Famous actresses getting treated like regular people? Mom smiles and whispers to me: "I love Wisconsin. Let's move here."

"Mom, your teeth are chattering."

"G-good point."

What can I say? We're solar-powered people.

Mom says, "Could you please go check on your sister, Jess? You know the way she feels about . . . this place."

Eva isn't handling Wisconsin very well. It's not the fact that we got stuck in a traffic jam caused by a cow, or that the mosquitoes are big enough to have their own landing lights. It's Wisconsin, the Badger State itself. My sister was up for the lead role in Sophie Cassala's *Wisconsin Girl*; E thought she had it locked. She never gave up thinking she had a shot at it—until a certain dreamy-eyed, pillow-lipped, blond movie star was confirmed for the part. (We try not to mention her name around E; hint: It's a synonym for crimson, red, and carmine.) This relocation adds geography to injury.

E is meeting with a reporter from the local paper, the *Post-Crescent*. Keiko has Eva fully prepped via e-mail, so E knows what to say about New London High School ("Go Dogs!") and the upcoming Water Street parade ("Wish I could be here!").

The mini-interview winds down. As the reporter leaves, Carlton arrives.

"Hi, Carlton." Dressed in his preppy uniform, Carlton approaches.

"Hi, Eva. Jessica."

"How's that spec script going?"

"Pretty good." Carlton's eyes dart over to me. "Some strong scenes. Working on the dialogue."

I get the strange impression that it's me Carlton wants to communicate with. Something that he doesn't want E to hear.

Eva's cell rings and she checks the number. "I've got to take this, but I'll be back." She heads around the corner to talk.

Carlton looks relieved to see her go. "Jessica," he says, pulling me behind a tall arrangement of brochures. "I overheard Murphy on his cell phone. He was planning something. And it sounds like sabotage."

I'll bet it did. I look Carlton right in the eye: "Tell me more."

scene 5

I'm about to (maybe) crack the case of Project Stop Skunk, but a little part of my brain can't help asking: Does Jeremy Jones *always* have to bust me with another guy? Jeremy enters the lobby to find Carlton and me tucked away in a corner together.

Carlton speaks in a low, urgent voice. "Look, we can't talk here. Can you meet me in the hotel gym in five minutes? The gym is closed, but the clerk told me the place is never locked."

It's hard to read his expression through his bulky, smudged glasses. I hesitate, then: "Okay."

"Jessica, please, don't tell anyone where you're going. I could get in big trouble for talking about a . . . friend of Lavender's."

"But wha—?"

Carlton doesn't seem to hear me. He brushes a palm leaf out of his way and heads down the hall. Jeremy has been pretending to review the Badger Inn activities board (*Happy Eightieth Birthday, Grandpa Clark*), but as soon as Carlton leaves, he rushes over to me. I don't even have a chance to step out from behind the brochures.

"Jessica, I have to talk to you."

"You do?"

"It's about Murphy."

Did Jeremy overhear something too? "What's going on?"

"It doesn't matter what's going on. Stay away from him."

Oh, I get it. "First, it's Alex. Now it's Murphy you don't want me talking to."

Jeremy's jaw clenches, tight. "Jessica, Murphy is trouble." His voice drops. "I got a text from a friend of mine who worked crew on *Crank Pranksters*. The guy who was Murphy's rival on the show wound up in a coma."

"A coma?"

"Something went wrong with a skydiving prank. They haven't been able to pin it on Murphy, but the police have been keeping an eye on him."

Ah. The secret reason that Lavender didn't want the police on the Warner Brothers set. The cops would have one more reason to hassle her boyfriend.

Eva pokes her head around the Huckleberry Campgrounds handouts. "Jessica, is this guy bothering you?"

"No."

"This guy?" Jeremy narrows his eyes. "Eva, we've worked together for a year."

You get demoted from friend to "this guy" with every sister-dumping. Get over it.

I tug Jeremy's sleeve. Focus. "Why hasn't anybody heard anything about the coma?"

"The show is hushing it up. They thought Murphy was about to be a breakout star before the accident—"

Eva interrupts. "Murphy had an accident?"

Eva's and Jeremy's cells ring at the same time. Jeremy has changed his ring from a song to a simple buzz.

"They're ready for us."

"E, do you have a few minutes . . . ?"

"Sorry, Jessica. We'll catch up later, okay?"

"Okay."

Now Mary from Makeup pokes her head in. "Eva, Jeremy, we need you *now*."

Mary is practically pulling Jeremy away from me and down the hall. "Stay away from him, Jessica. Promise me?"

I don't know how he does it. But somehow the guy makes me feel sad that I have to tell him, "No, Jeremy. I can't."

I rush out of the lobby toward the gym. Jeremy isn't the only one running late.

scene 6

The strategy: Go right to an abandoned corridor of the hotel. Meet a guy I barely know. Don't tell anyone. While a bunch of suspicious activities are going on around the set.

173

Yikes—not a perfect plan. I text Mom to let her know where I'm headed, and to expect me back in ten minutes.

I had hoped Eva would come with me, or at least play lookout, but no luck. And yet, I don't want to not show up: this could be the opportunity to narrow down my sabotage suspects from two to one.

From Murphy to Carlton.

Or from Carlton to Murphy.

Murphy has the skills to pull off all the pranks—and the bad attitude. Then there's the housekeeper clue. If Rita was honest about not selling me out, then Murphy is the most likely person to have told Roman that someone had been let into the room. Though there's always a possibility that someone else saw me go into the room. Motive? Hmm . . . the skunking could have been revenge for Lavender getting passed over by MTV, but the other pranks have hurt more than helped her.

Carlton—I don't know what sabotage abilities he has. But if he's a guy who's always pitching new ideas, then maybe the *Skunk'd* proposal was his—it was in his bag. And since the writers are the first to know where *Two Sisters* will be shooting, he'd have the opportunity to make trouble before anyone else was on the scene. Motive? He would have footage for his new *Skunk'd* show, and in the meantime, he has also looked smart and "quick" with all his postprank rewrites.

So the gym meeting is my chance to see if Carlton has information on Murphy—or to get a firsthand look at Carlton's next move.

How much trouble do I want to take on to get that look?

I mentally review my mom's Stranger Danger tips. She made me study these after my run-in with the set thief a couple of weeks ago.

⭐ **Be aware of your surroundings.**

⭐ **The first thing to do when in danger: Run away! Scream for help!**

⭐ **Never let yourself be taken to a second location.**

⭐ **The eyes are the most vulnerable part of the body. Poke him there.**

⭐ **The knee is the strongest point on the body. If you are close enough to use it, do!**

I put my hand in my jean pocket, ready to press Mom's speed-dial number. With my other hand, I push into the gym.

Carlton is standing in the middle of the mirrored room surrounded by exercise bikes and a collection of intimidating silver machines with oddly placed seats. Some weights lie on the ground. A huge floor-to-ceiling window lets in the late-morning light at the opposite side of the room. "You came. I wasn't sure you would."

Neither was I. "What did you want to tell me?"

"I overheard Murphy on the phone. It sounded like he was planning another prank." As Carlton talks, he walks over to the window. I stay where I am—close to the exit. "I can't accuse a friend of Lavender's, but you don't work for the show. And you caught that set thief. From what I heard, the view from this room . . . *waitaminute!*" Carlton has spotted something out the window. Or at least he acts like he has. He takes off his glasses to clean them on his shirt. "Jessica, come look. What's going on?"

I edge away from the door, but not exactly toward the window.

Carlton looks at me. "What? You don't trust me?" He squints. "Is this because I never got back to you about your TV idea? I mean, you stole my bag to slip me the idea, so you must think it's pretty great, but a skunk-and-camera concept? Never fly."

"I stole your . . . ? What?" I start moving toward the window but keep one eye on the now-insanely-rambling Carlton. I peek outside.

Carlton points below. "That can't be right. Right?"

I look. I see. I run.

There isn't even time to apologize to Carlton for doubting him.

scene 7

The view from the gym revealed a row of cars at rest, and one saboteur at work. I race down the Badger Inn hallways, and push open the double doors onto the parking lot.

I only hope I'm not . . .

I am.

I *so* am.

Too late.

Murphy is almost done with his work. He's wrapping a huge pink truck in some kind of plastic. He's sabotaging the set vehicles!

"Stop! Stop!" I cry, launching myself at Murphy.

"Hey!" he yells. I give him a taste of Abuela's iron grip, and quickly have him down on the ground. With his arms caught between us, I try wrapping his wrists in the heavy-duty plastic wrap. But by then my element of surprise is gone, and Murphy's element of being twice my size starts to kick in. The only reason I'm holding my own is that he's got one hand on his trucker hat. Someone must have broken it to him about the cornrows. We're rolling around on the ground in a pile of plastic when suddenly we hear the Mouth from the South.

"Oh, no! Mah Stomperado monster truck has been covered in plastic wrap! How can Ah get to its roomy leather interior, surround sound stereo, and exemplary trunk space?"

Can you believe it? Murphy was sabotaging his own girlfriend! Or is it *faux*friend?

"Lavender, help!" I shout. "I caught the saboteur!"

Lavender looks at me over the top of her dark shades.

I notice that she is shivering in a new Marc Jacobs purple sundress and matching kitten heels. It's the first time I've seen her without her long jacket since we hit Wisconsin. Her hair is super-glossy, and her face is coated in heavy, camera-ready makeup.

I'm not Eva's sister for nothing. I can recognize when an actress has been prepped to take the stage.

Belatedly, too-latedly, I realize: I just stole the limelight from Lavender's reality show debut! She had been in on the prank—ready to "Oh, me, oh, mah!" her way into reality TV history.

Obviously, the scene was about as spontaneous as the Stomperado commercial that it really was. I guess I don't have to ask who is sponsoring the show.

I've got pink plastic wrap around my ears, but when Lavender bends over me, I'm pretty sure I hear her right: "*This* is why Ah don't know who you are!"

"I'm sorry, Lavender. Carlton overheard . . . well, we made a mistake." Or was it just me who made the mistake—in trusting him?

"Carlton? That guy who is always hanging around Lavvy?" Murphy's voice is low and rough. Our eyes lock. The look he gives me cuts sharper than the Wisconsin wind. I have the feeling I couldn't have said a name that would have made him angrier.

I head to the conference room where the *Two Sisters* cast and crew are gathered.

Time to explain to Carlton that he had misunderstood Murphy's phone call. (Or time to pull every perfectly prepped hair out of his head if he set me up. I'm hoping the answer will show on his face.) I also need to explain to my mom the new collection of scrapes on my arms.

The writers are revising dialogue with Eva and Jeremy. Mom is listening in; I wave to her. Beside me, I overhear Paige on her cell. "No, not the Hogan bag, the Carlton bag! Mom and I each have to have one. It's the new It Bag!"

Uh-oh. As usual, Paige's fashion sense is malfunctioning.

"The Jennifers have it! So I have to have it. Stop talking and just get it!"

I don't especially want to rescue Paige from her mistake, but the poor assistant on the other end of the line shouldn't be looking for a bag that doesn't exist.

Paige clicks off her phone.

"Paige, the Carlton isn't a kind of bag. Carlton is one of the writers on the show. He had his name embroidered on his bag."

Paige pulls out her compact and starts applying lip gloss. "You think you're smarter than me, don't you?"

Where did that come from? (Besides Truthville.) "Fine. Forget it."

Sorry I tried to help.

If that assistant has any smarts, she's home sewing C-A-R-L-T-O-N onto pink plaid right now.

"Look, Shirley Sherlock, that preppy writer isn't the person who was so desperate to get his hands on the bag."

If he wasn't, then . . . ?

At that moment, Anxious Al makes an announcement, telling everyone the real reason we're in Wisconsin.

And the real reason that I have to avoid the set at all costs.

scene 8

I blow it. Again.

Mom and I are in our room at the Badger Inn. Mom is reviewing the latest script changes—the ones that say "Scarlett Johansson" where it used to say "Very Special Guest Star." Scarlett Johansson is shooting on location. She's the real reason we're in Wisconsin: filming here while she's shooting *Wisconsin Girl* was the only way to fit into her schedule.

"Mom, I can't go to the set. I mean, I won't. I shouldn't."

"Now, Jess, you can't put off what you want to do because of talk about a jinx. If you start now . . . well, you're not going to start now. You said you *can't* go to the set; you didn't say you didn't want to. I'm afraid you won't believe you can unless you do."

I don't want to go to the set. Why is that so hard to remember? After all, with two angry actresses, an angry producer, an angry practical joker, an ex-almost-boyfriend, and a bad-luck streak with visiting celebs . . . would *you* want to go to the set?

More importantly, I know who the saboteur is, and I've got to find the evidence to get him.

Well, it's too late now—for me, and for the lovely Scarlett Johansson, this episode's Very Special Guest Star. The addition of Scarlett to the episode was Anxious Al's announcement. Greeted with cheers from the room. And a few concerned looks my way.

Mom and I walk down the hallway to a Badger Inn conference room. *Two Sisters* is taking over the space, decorating it like a doll collectors' convention. Scarlett plays an avid doll collector who has inadvertently adopted a petnapped dog.

When I arrive at the back of the room, Al twitches his eye at me. "Isn't it great that Scarlett could do the part? She's in the area filming a Sophie Cassala movie."

I know I speak for my sister when I say: *Yippee.*

I try to lie low, but the truth is: Scarlett could not be more fantastic. She admires my new wool sweater, remembers my name, and splits the last double-glazed doughnut with me.

I head farther off by myself, behind the man-high piles of lumber the crew has brought in. If my staying away increases Scarlett's chances of an accident-free acting experience, that's what I want.

Unfortunately, two other people are lying low too. Or at least, lying.

I don't see them, tucked around a corner of a "Famous Dolls in History" booth, but I recognize his low voice and her Southern drawl.

"And you have so got that Halle Berry thing going on."

Oh, he did *not* go there.

Carlton is laying his sorry rap on Lavender, and she seems to be interested.

"You'd be surprised how many people tell me that, shug."

I'd be surprised, all right.

"I was thinking of Halle for this movie I'm writing, but you would be such a better fit."

I'm about to have a fit myself, but I don't want to do anything to attract the jinx gods. You know, if I believed in them.

"Ah've had this idea for a one-woman show, *Are You There God? It's Me, Lavender*."

"One word," says Carlton confidently. "Genius."

The word I was thinking was: *Aggh!*

Are you there God? I think I'm going to be ill.

If Lavender is here keeping Carlton busy, then where is Murphy?

I need to find out.

Now.

Right now.

I leave the construction area and head to the Craft Services table, where my sister is loading up on ice cream.

I'm kidding. Water.

Eva notices her producer enter the room. "Um, Jessica, any reason that Roman is giving you a death stare?"

"He probably just has something in his eye."

Like the desire to sentence me to Siberia.

Thank you, Alex Banks.

"Attention!" Roman calls. I think the same thing I always do when I look at him now: Hess, Kess, Less, Mess? "We're ready for a script read. Ms. Johansson?"

Scarlett and Paige have been chatting in the corner and now approach the read-through table.

That's when I spot him.

He spots me, too. And doesn't look happy to see me.

Embarrass, ruin, and wrestle with a guy right before trying to worm into his good graces—not my best plan. But it's the only one I've got.

Act V

A lot of people are afraid to say what they want.
That's why they don't get what they want.

—MADONNA

"*Y*ou will not know the day or the hour when disaster will strike."

"Yeah, I never do. Sorry again, Murphy."

Murphy is getting right in my face. The brim of his trucker hat juts toward my forehead. "Lav and I were both gonna get Stomperados if that scene went on *Crank Pranksters*."

So they weren't just rehearsing, but then . . . "Where were the cameras?"

Murphy runs a hand over the big black circle on the front of his hat. He doesn't answer, but he does change his tune faster than an iPod click. His voice turns confidential, and, for him, quiet. "Look, Jessica, I know that you were set up."

"You do?"

He motions me into the hallway.

"That Stomperado disaster—it was a frame-up. And Carlton was behind it."

"Maybe he misunderstood—"

"Please. He's too smart for that. He wants to make sure that you and I are the main suspects for the sabotage. We're obvious targets anyway."

I nod.

"After the inking and dognapping, Carlton's brainstorms won him points with the boss, and put him on the fast track to head writer. He's been setting the sabotage to make himself look good. But I've got a way to catch him." He narrows his eyes at me. "You in?"

I gulp. Murphy is seriously spooky when he smiles. "You have a plan?"

"Watch me."

"Quit watching me."

"Sorry."

"These are pranking trade secrets."

I texted Mom my location. Now I'm on lookout. Murphy is kneeling outside a hotel door. He says he's got a secret way to get us into Carlton's room. To me, it looks like he got Carlton's room key somehow.

"We'll get the evidence and get out," Murphy says.

I reach into my pocket, fingers on my cell. I'm calling for help if things get weird.

Well, weirder.

"We're in." The door handle turns under Murphy's fingers.

The door hangs open, and Murphy and I are both exposed and guilty-looking in the hallway. I don't hurry into the room. There is still a mental wall against sneaking into someone's space. A moral struggle, and let's face it . . . I don't want to be in a room with Murphy by myself. Even if Mom is only a speed-dial away.

He pushes past me into the room. I take a deep breath. I follow. The door closes behind me with a click.

The room is a twin of Eva's deluxe suite. Big bed, TV, nightstand, table with a laptop, closet. The air is sweet. The closet is closed with a clunky gold lock.

Murphy points. "Look under the bed." He heads for the laptop, which is sitting open and turned on.

"How much time do we have?" I ask.

"I don't know. Maybe ten minutes?" Or twenty. Or two. Shoots are unpredictable; that door handle could start turning any second. "No exit."

He's right. There's no sliding door to a patio here. Murphy and I could hide in the bathroom, but that would only buy us a few minutes. We'd be trapped.

I kneel on the floor and look around. I see a bulky duffel bag. Not the pink Carlton bag; one I haven't seen before.

Open it, Jessica. Open it.

Gently, I tug the zipper. Then I see red. The color of a jacket. And it's not a preppy-approved gingham red. It's the same shade as my Academy jacket.

Murphy's still at the keyboard. *Tap-tap-tap-tap-tap.*

I know that anyone could want a new jacket—I mean, "red is the new red." But none of that explains the ponytail.

At the bottom of the bag is a bunch of fake brown hair bound to look like a ponytail. Why would anyone have this?

Answer: to sabotage the set—and try to blame it on me. Again.

"Look at this!" Murphy points excitedly to the laptop. I shove the jacket and ponytail into the bag. Then I look over Murphy's shoulder. A list of file names comes up on the screen.

AfterInkOut.doc
AfterMissingDog.doc
AftertheFire.doc

The files are all dated from before each incident of sabotage. A saboteur would be able to prepare scripts to deal with the "surprises" and have brilliant brainstorms all thought out. But wait. . . .

"Murphy, click on 'After the Fire.'" *Two Sisters* hasn't had a fire. Yet.

The page opens. Murphy leans close to the screen, blocking my view. "It's about Scarlett's dress! It's rigged to go up in flames. In the scene she's shooting now!"

scene 2

*M*urphy and I abandon Carlton's room. By the time I wonder if we should have grabbed the bag of evidence and the laptop, the door has already slammed behind us.

At first, Murphy is in the lead, but I'm gaining on him. When we hit the shooting area, I'm the first one through the doors.

That's why I'm the first one on top of Scarlett.

People seemed like they were frozen in slow motion as I hurried by them. Lavender beaming to be in a scene with Scarlett. Jeremy holding Mr. Ruffs. Tommy the Pet-Man giving Mr. Ruffs his signals. Paige and Eva looking at the dolls that decorate the set. Extras pretending to be perusing the booths. Crew, led by Roman, monitoring all technical aspects. Proud moms, mine and Paige's, on the sideline. Mama Paige holds Tink on her lap.

I passed by them all.

If they shouted, I never heard it.

If they grabbed for me, I never felt it.

Like a football player in the end zone, I made my tackle.

Scarlett's ever-drowsy eyes widened; her full lips parted. Then she hit the ground.

"The dress! We've got to get the dress off her! Fire!" I pull and tear at the dress.

Then I do hear shouting. And feel hands. Roman's hands. He pulls me off Scarlett. "What's going on? What are you doing, you maniac!"

I try to explain. I try to catch my breath. "Scarlett's dress. Going to burn."

"Are you threatening me? You are off my set forever! Call the police on this little—"

Mom jumps in. She stands between me and Roman. "Give her a minute! Let her explain."

Roman doesn't want to hear it. He gives Mom his full-blown death glare, known to leave studio executives and their story suggestions huddled in a corner, sobbing and broken. "You had better get her out of here if you don't want to take me on."

Mom makes her choice: *"If!"*

Behind me, I can hear Hélène helping Scarlett repair her dress.

"There's no time for this!" I shout. "Scarlett's dress is rigged. Ask Murphy."

"Murphy?" says Lavender, surprised. "Where's Murphy?"

I look around. Murphy is nowhere in sight.

And I know deep in my rapidly beating heart: I just got played.

Rita's last words to me at the hotel: *"La verdad padece pero no perece."*

My Spanish wasn't good enough to translate on the spot, but I Googled the words later. A Mexican proverb: The truth suffers but never perishes.

The truth will come out. I believe that. But I'd sure appreciate a rough estimate of how much suffering has to come first.

Jeremy looks worried. "What does this have to do with Murphy? I told you to stay away from him."

"You told her *what*?" Lavender says.

Scarlett is still in her dress. And it might be rigged to burst into flames.

But then again, I have only Murphy's word on that.

Of course, Murphy *is* the set saboteur, so who would know better than him?

I knew Carlton was not behind the pranks, but if you were me, what would you have done? In my mind, I replay all the evidence that points to Murphy's guilt.

Paige had busted Murphy. He got caught planting the *Skunk'd* proposal in Carlton's bag, and convinced her the Carlton was the new It Bag.

Next, Murphy had known which door was Mr. Ruffs's at Hotel Banks—even though he'd told me he hadn't been to that part of the hotel before. It's hard to remember what you're not supposed to know.

But I wasn't sure—not completely—till I went into the hotel room with Murphy. That's why I had to go. And nothing about the place was right. It was a room as nice as Eva's—a top-of-the-food-chain suite. Not one for a junior writer. And who would go to the trouble of locking his closet, then put the incriminating evidence under the bed? Murphy was locking Lavender's things out of sight. And the smell in the room? Lavender might not remember my name, but I'd know her scent anywhere.

Murphy didn't need to know a "pranking trade secret" to bust into the room. It was Lavender's room. He had the key all along.

Why set me up as a Scarlett-attacker and Carlton as the saboteur? Maybe Murphy didn't like how much time Carlton was spending with his girlfriend? Maybe he wanted to get me off his trail. And if he didn't like us to begin with—that Stomperado disaster? Didn't help.

As for the chewed-up Jessica bracelet? Hmm . . . that's a loose end. Did he send that as a warning?

I focus back on real time.

Jeremy, Lavender, Eva, and Paige are in one cluster facing me and Mom, who are faced off against Roman. Scarlett is off to the side with Hélène—and yes, most of the male crew, who are offering their assistance to the beautiful movie star. Carlton, Anxious Al, and Amber hurry over.

"Please." I have to try again. "There were scripts. Scripts about each of the sabotage attacks. The last one was called 'After the Fire.' About Scarlett's dress."

Hélène presses my shoulder. "I sewed Ms. Johansson's dress myself, and I checked it again now. There is nothing wrong with the dress. Nothing flammable. I promise you."

So there was never a flaming dress. But there might have been.

You see why I had to do what I did? There was no time to find out if the prank was dangerous to Scarlett, or if it was all a setup to have me flinging myself onto the scene and accusing Carlton.

I'm relieved the dress is safe, even though it means it isn't evidence for my accusation.

If volcanoes had a voice right before they blew, they would sound like Roman. "Mrs. Ortiz, you have one minute to get your younger daughter out of here."

"**D**id I miss anything?" Murphy arrives.

"What kept you?"

"I tripped." He gives a sly half grin, not even trying to make me believe the lie. He slants a glance at Carlton. "What'd Jessica say happened?"

I stare into Murphy's brown eyes. "I'm telling the truth. *You* are behind all the trouble. You've been recording all our accidents to air on your creepy *Crank Pranksters* show."

No cameras at the Stomperado "commercial" meant Murphy had some seriously secret ways to film the action. I'm just guessing on this. But it's a good guess that gives him a serious motive. . . .

Murphy looks genuinely surprised. That I caught him. "Strong accusation, Jess. Got proof?"

"The proof is all on the laptop that you left in the room. *Lavender's* room."

Lavender is surprised. "*Mah* room?"

Jeremy moves to put his arm around me. Mom and Eva are on my other side. "Should we go to Lavender's room, Murphy? Now? You can explain why there's a laptop, a wig, and a red jacket there."

"Red? Ah never wear red." Lavender is a few beats behind.

Murphy doesn't answer. He smiles his big, spooky grin.

Lighting Guy Bob says, "I found a minicamera set up in the hamster cage prop. Thought maybe I missed a meeting with the camera crew."

Roman grits his teeth. "So all the hassle has been for some TV show? And we're being recorded now?"

Murphy smirks. He takes off his trucker hat to reveal that it's run through with wires: a portable camera. "Smile, Roman. You're on Cranky Camera."

"But how did you . . . ?" Roman pauses. Then he screws on a thin smile, growling, "You're in big trouble, babe."

"Don't think so, *babe*. *Two Sisters* and *Crank Pranksters* are both owned by Banks Brothers. My stunts were approved from the top. A little cross-promotion—good for both our ratings. Especially since *Snake Bait* took a bite out of yours."

Murphy pulls a photo from his back pocket. In it Ivan Banks has his arm around him, giving a big thumbs-up.

And then Roman . . . screams? Throttles Murphy? Explodes?

None of the above.

He turns his back.

And that's when it sinks in: Murphy is going to get away with it. The skunking, the inking, the petnapping, the *everything*.

Murphy stuffs the photo back in his pocket. He starts to stride off, but turns back to announce, "Don't worry about how we'll edit my show, everybody. Ron Howard couldn't take better care of you." Is that a promise or a threat?

I'm practically expecting a slug trail to slime behind Murphy, but everyone else snaps back to business, fast. If there are undercurrents of concern, it's more about how Murphy will feature people on his show, not about how he crossed all the lines of normal behavior. That's showbiz?

Roman shouts out orders. "Lighting Guy Bob, find every minicamera and get them out of here. Actors, take your places."

I have to face up to what I did.

"I'm so sorry, Scarlett." Jeremy comes up beside me. He doesn't say a word, just puts his hand on my elbow, showing support.

"It's okay."

Scarlett's lips say okay. Her eyes say "Stay back, foaming-mouthed insaniac." She has very expressive eyes.

"Are you sure you're all right?"

"Just a scratch. Makeup can cover it up." Scarlett holds up her palm; there is a thin mark from where her hand hit the ground.

All eyes are on Scarlett, oohing and aahing over her injury.

All I can think is . . . my jinx is lessening! We're down to scratches! Not counting dress-tearing attacks! We're down to scratches! Everything is going to be . . .

C
R
A
S
H
!

Everyone had been watching Scarlett when a speaker crashed from the overhead rigging to the floor.

And stretched out on the ground next to the speaker is Paige. Her eyes are closed, her breathing looks shallow.

What happened?

Did the speaker hit her on the way down?

The crew rushes to Paige's side. "She's breathing!" the head cameraman says.

Paige's eyes flicker. She moans quietly, and holds her forehead. Her mom takes a look at her injured daughter and screams, "Why? Why does everything happen to *me*?"

Mama Paige faints into Jeremy's arms.

Scarlett dials 911 on her cell.

Lighting Guy Bob is fanning Paige with his clipboard.

Eva gets out her phone. I think she's calling an ambulance, but I quickly realize she's dialed Keiko. "Jess, can you go to the hospital to help with Paige? I'd go myself, but I have to work up a message for the press saying how concerned I am about her."

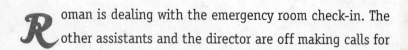

*R*oman is dealing with the emergency room check-in. The other assistants and the director are off making calls for

Paige. My mom is watching Tink; I think she thought it would be awkward to mother Paige while her own mother is on the scene. That leaves me to listen to Paige screaming over her cell phone. "Remy, get over here now! You can't believe the room they have me in! It's like a third world prison!"

Actually, we're still in the waiting area—which is an entirely nondescript white room with plastic chairs. The room smells like bleach and blue soap covering another smell that I don't want to think about.

Like everyone who's ever been to an ER, I don't want to look around in case someone's hideously wounded . . . but yet I must. Nope, everyone looks pretty much okay—the worst expressions of pain are on the faces of the nurses who are approaching Paige.

The staff gathers around, gently helping Paige toward a wheelchair. The fact that she practically wrestles one of the male nurses to the ground to get a slightly newer wheelchair does not stem their concern for her fragile health.

As Paige loudly berates the staff, I find myself discreetly apologizing for her.

"What are you whispering? What are you saying? It better be that I need a new pillow and a bottle of Fiji water."

Paige is assigned a private room. She complains violently when helped from her wheelchair. She's given a small pill for the pain. If only doctors could prescribe a dose of reality.

"Owwwww . . ." She's flailing about in the hospital bed. She looks around. "I've died. I've died, and . . ." She glares at me. ". . . gone straight to . . ."

She doesn't say heaven. I'd like to blame the medication she is on, but that charm . . . that's so Paige.

It doesn't matter. My mind is miles from here—racing with possibilities.

Was the falling speaker a last setup by Murphy? He denied it, but he's fluent in lying. Yet none of the other pranks would have seriously injured anyone—this feels different.

The timing is too insane for a coincidence. Isn't it?

Which leaves me with this thought: jinx?

That's what I'm thinking when the door swings open and Jeremy arrives.

My heart does a double-skip, the traitor.

"Jess . . . ," he says, surprised to see me.

"*There* you are, Remy. Did you walk backwards to get here? Jessica has been begging them for water and an extra pillow for me, but these doctors don't know how to treat people."

"Sorry, Paige. I got held up with your mom." Jeremy turns to ask what I'm doing there.

"Everyone else is dealing with phone calls, publicity control, paperwork." *And hiding from Paige's family drama.*

"Where's my mom?" Paige asks.

"She's trying to get admitted to the hospital for shock," Jeremy says.

"I'll give her a shock," Paige growls. I think Mama and Paige have switched from buddies back to battling.

I've never seen Jeremy look so strained. "Thanks, Jess. It was kind of you to wait here."

Paige's eyes are swinging between us. She doesn't like what she sees. A quick exit is called for.

"Feel better," I tell her, ducking out of the room.

I'm heading out of the hospital when I pass the gift shop. I can see they are selling bottles of Evian and a small pillow that says IT'S A GIRL on it.

I decide to have the water and pillow sent up to Paige. Not because we're going to be friends any time soon. Just because it's what my mom would have done for me.

Dear lovely Ms. Scarlett,

Actress and star,

Whose talent and beauty

Will be taking her far . . .

So sorry for jumping

On top of your dress

The tearing and pulling

Caused you distress.

Please know I regret

Every moment and minute

Especially as (re: the dress)

You were in it.

*M*y apology poem complete, I'm writing a letter to my *abuela*. I am sitting on a bench in Franklin Park, enjoying a spot in Wisconsin where the sun feels *strong*. My bones are warming up.

I'm making a list for Abuela of my favorite things about New London, Wisconsin. "At the car wash, you don't get acting resumes slipped to you by the soap dudes; you get . . . your car washed. The men in 4x4s are farmers, not stalkerazzi. They have a historical marker for the Wisconsin state dog (American water spaniel) at the park. They have the nicest expression for telling you that your ideas are crazy: 'Well, that's different.'"

"Who are you writing to?" I didn't see Jeremy come into the park, but he's suddenly standing next to my bench.

"My *abuela*."

Jeremy seems relieved for some reason. "You were great to stay with Paige."

"Is she all right?"

"Yeah, she was just shaken up. Actually the network lawyer looked like he was in worse shape. He found out that Paige had sued her manicurist over a chipped nail or something, and he freaked. He's over there ordering massages and special therapies for her and Tink right now."

I want to say: *Why aren't you there too? It's where you belong*.

But instead, I say: "Well, I'll see you."

I want him to go, but instead Jeremy sits down beside me. "Did you get the bracelet?"

Way to rub it in. *No, I didn't get the Tiffany's bracelet. Paige did.* "No," I say sharply.

"What?" Jeremy looks concerned. "When I found it with Mr. Ruffs, I packed it in a *Two Sisters* box and sent it to your room."

Oh.

That bracelet.

Paige gets a Tiffany's silver bracelet, and I get a dog's chew toy.

"*You* sent me the Jessica bracelet?" I admit it: the Jeremy effect makes my detective powers go a little wonky.

He nods. "I thought you knew that. I asked at Paige's party if you got my 'message.' I didn't want to say that I found the bracelet with Mr. Ruffs. It might have looked weird for you."

"Why didn't you put your name on the box?"

"I wasn't sure you'd open it if you thought it was from me."

"Oh."

Had we moved *that* far apart? I guess we had.

"Jessica, I'm sorry. I had a bad case of the stupids. Can you forgive me?"

"What for?" I ask.

Okay.

Okay.

Okay.

You know that usually—almost always—I'm above cheap girlfriend tests, like making the guy guess the *real* reason I'm mad, but this time I had to know that he knows. Or else he might do it again.

Jeremy looks me right in the eyes. "For hurting your feelings," he says simply.

He knows.

I look down at my hands, which somehow he is holding in both of his. "Jess, I've never had a life outside of working—not ever. When I see the flashes go off, I do what the camera wants me to do." He squeezes my fingers. "That's all I was doing with Paige at the fashion show. Then you broke up with me, Paige was all over me. . . . I wanted you to know that's how it all happened." So Paige only became Jeremy's girlfriend because he thought that I was with "Heathcliff." That's when one kiss-for-the-camera turned into a rebound girlfriend.

I don't say anything; I look down at our joined hands.

Jeremy stumbles on. "So how much do you hate me?"

"I don't hate you." And now I have to say something out loud—something that I didn't even want to admit in my own thoughts. I stare straight at my shoes as I say, "You didn't kiss me like that." I dare a peek up at Jeremy's face. He looks surprised. "You know," I ramble miserably, "with the dipping and the hair and everything."

"Jess, what are you talking about?"

I don't answer. I've said everything I'm going to about this gut-clenchingly embarrassing topic. So Jeremy says, "I thought the dip would work better for the camera angle, and the hands-in-the-hair thing . . . I don't know—I was on a soap opera when I was a kid. They did a lot of that."

I keep looking at the ground. Maybe I can stare a bottomless hole into it and step in.

Jeremy tips my chin up so that I have to look at him. But I won't look into his eyes . . . his big, blue, sincere . . . too late.

When he speaks again, it's in a quiet voice, and I can feel his breath on my face. "I was thinking about how the kiss looked on camera with that stuff, Jessica. When I kiss you, everything is too . . . real. I don't think at all." He leans closer to my face. "Except about how pretty you are." And closer. "And how much I like you." And closer. "And how much I'd like to kiss you again."

Then he is kissing me again.

It's Jeremy. So it's wonderful.

"Be my date for the wrap party," he says between kisses. I shake my head, trying to clear all the zinging. "C'mon, Jess," he says, smiling, but worried, too. "If you can kiss me like that and still be mad, then you're a better actress than your sister."

I pull away from him. "Are you telling me that you broke up with a girl who is in the hospital?"

Jeremy's face gets real red, real fast. "Uh . . . she's resting back at her room."

As if Paige's exact location was what I was asking him.

"And, no . . . no, I didn't find the exact right moment to say . . . you know . . . goodbye."

Really? No good dump-off spots between her hospital bed and the nurses' checkout area. Who's surprised?

Maybe it isn't exactly as though Jeremy is checking to see if I'm available, even if he's not. Maybe it's not quite that. But it's still not right.

"Thanks for the apology, Jeremy. It meant a lot. And I'm sorry too. For the way I've acted. For the stuff my sister . . . for the stuff I let my sister say."

Now I'd like to tell you that I walk away.

Shoulders back, head high, without a backward glance.

Instead, there may be a brief hug with hospital-girl's boyfriend (and a surreptitious breathing-in of his T-shirt's compelling detergent-clean-meets-irresistible-guy smell), but then I do go.

And I don't look back.

Even when he asks, "And who's this Heathcliff anyway?"

scene 6

*M*om and I are wearing foam-rubber slices of cheese on our heads. No, Paige's bad fashion fever isn't catching, we're dressed like Green Bay Packers fans. We're seated as extras on the fifty-yard line at Lambeau Field watching actors in Packers uniforms hurl a football.

The big "Ruffs Reunion" scene is set up for filming. Waiting for the shooting to begin, I reach into my bag (all right . . . Eva's bag that I'm borrowing and will return in perfect, practically-wasn't-even-borrowed condition). I hand Mom a present.

"Oh, a book!" she says happily. You can take the mom out of the library, but you can't take, etc.

Murphy the Mook did serve one good purpose. A name he mentioned gave me a clue to solving another mystery: how to help Mom get her cool back. She reads the title: *Ron Howard: From Mayberry to the Moon . . . and Beyond.*

"Ooh, I'll look forward to reading this."

I hope *Opie* will help calm some of Mom's worries. Some young actors aren't "scarred and scared" by their experiences. And if that book doesn't do it, I've got *Leonardo DiCaprio: From* Growing Pains *to King of the World* and *Jodie Foster: Actress, Yalie, Director, Mom.*

"I guess you're tired of my athletic phase." Is it only a librarian who would think reading sports parenting books was an "athletic phase"? "I'm just exploring ways to process what's happening to our family. Especially since my formerly quiet daughter is now involved with her own dramas." Mom takes my hands. "Jessica, you know you don't have to be like Eva to be powerful and interesting, right?"

"Why would I think that? *Waitaminute!* Should I think that?"

Mom's face crumbles like blue cheese.

Too easy.

"Sorry, Mom. Couldn't resist!"

She starts to breathe again, and manages a tiny smile. "Enjoy your children, the first rule of parenting." Her eyes narrow. "I wish you many daughters."

Somehow it doesn't seem quite like a blessing with that peculiar expression on her face.

We hear the always-bracing cry of "Action!"

Eva enters stage left. Her bright blue sundress flares around her as she rushes forward, gripping her cheese-hat to her head.

"Mr. Ruffs's twin! Is it truly you?" E throws her arm around the cocker spaniel, burying her face in his soft neck. Now, I fully know that E does not like dogs (chewing-burying-scratching-embarrassing leg-attackers is her misguided thinking), but even I'm tearing up. The girl is good! Mr. Ruffs's performance is spot-on, too.

Mom is suddenly looking at the real reason that she let her daughter get into the whole crazy business. My sister loves acting, and when she's acting she's happy, and when she's happy . . . she's beautiful.

Eva loves every piece of acting—figuring out the character from the inside out, getting into someone else's clothes and into their skin. She loves making up her character's backstory, wearing her character's pajamas to bed at night, and writing her diary in her character's voice.

I never said she wasn't straight-up strange.

My mom would stand between Eva and a world of trouble, but, I suddenly realize, she couldn't bring herself to stand between E and what she loves.

Interesting.

So . . . what do I want Mom to let *me* do?

Maybe it's seeing all the twelve-year-olds driving tractors around here that has transportation on my mind, but I have to wonder . . . can I convince Mom in a couple of years that a learner's permit and a hot red convertible are *my* one true ticket to happy-beautiful?

scene 7

The *Two Sisters* producers have knocked themselves out putting together the end-of-shooting party. White tents are set up on the grounds off the Badger Inn's party room.

Colorful paper lanterns swing in the breeze. There's a polka band, a barbecue, and the best in Wisconsin catering, from cream puffs to bratwurst.

"I've tasted *wurst*," jokes Anxious Al. He can laugh after Roman's announcement.

"Al Maggio is moving into brand-new, bigger offices back at the lot. After all, anyone can write 'Save Me, Mr. Ruffs.' But who can get Scarlett Johansson to say it?" Pause. "Where's Scarlett?"

It turns out that Al's sister is a superagent in Hollywood, and all the top-notch guest stars that the show has attracted have been because of her pull.

Roman looks around. "Has anyone seen our Very Special Guest Star?"

I'll tell you a secret: I'm here. So Scarlett is not.

Maybe you wouldn't have played it like I did. Maybe you would have thought: None of the other pranks was deadly, why would this one be? Instead of tackling Scarlett, you might have found a soothing way of warning her about her imminent ignition. In which case, you're a faster thinker than I am.

How nice to be you.

Roman thanks the cast and crew for their hard work. He makes a few small jokes that get big laughs—perk of being the boss, I guess. Then various writers and crew members gather around him, but he pushes past everyone. He heads straight over to talk to the one person most surprised to get his attention.

Me.

"Hi, Roman."

He nods. But doesn't speak. He looks uncomfortable—awkward, even. So different from his usual world-beater attitude.

I realize: It can't be easy thanking me for catching Murphy after Roman confessed all those bad feelings he'd had about me, and then we had that weird Alex moment. He shifts uneasily from foot to foot. I plunge in, to help him out. "It wasn't anything much. Just happy it all worked out. Nice of you to come talk to me."

"You're standing in front of the men's room."

Oh.

Understood.

We'll bond later.

It's a big party—the Wisconsin extras are invited, the local press, and I think Grandpa Clark of Badger Inn bulletin board fame and his eightieth birthday party pals just crashed—but all I can see is a brown adhesive bandage.

The bandage is stuck to Paige's forehead; her hair is scraped back in a ponytail to draw attention to her injury. After all that screaming, the proper medical response to Paige's injury was deemed to be: a Band-Aid. And not one of those official square- or butterfly-shaped ones—a regular old rectangular one, like the kind that sometimes have pictures of *Sesame Street* characters.

Man, I wish hers had an Elmo on it.

Paige is clinging to Jeremy. Every time he looks like he might take a step away from her, she touches her Band-Aid and leans on his arm. And I thought she overacted in that spicy-hot tortilla commercial.

Jeremy catches my eye, and it's . . . okay.

We share a look. We share something . . . what's his word? . . . real. I could never ask him about the kite bracelet, but I would guess the kite is floating where it floated yesterday. Jeremy's feelings about me never changed.

Of course, now Paige isn't even wearing the bracelet. She's on the outs with her mom for selling *The National Enquirer* the story about her accident: "One Mother, One Heartache: Crumpled Paige!!!" Instead of a mom, Paige has a flock of studio lawyers twittering around her. "More Evian, Paige? *Please don't sue us for reckless set management.* More crudité, Paige? *Please don't sue us for endangering your life.*"

At her table, Mom has her book open to chapter three: "From

Happy Days to Happier Days," but I know she's been watching me.

"If that boy was bothering you . . ." Mom squints at Jeremy's departing back.

"It's cool, Mom. We're friends." Mom's face freezes. I can see it is taking every ounce of her mom-strength to submerge her disapproval.

Bow-wow! Jeremy is still in the doghouse with Mom.

Time to change the subject. . . .

"Mom, the reason you let Eva go to Hollywood with her acting . . . it's because she loves it, yes?"

Mom looks wary. "Yeees."

"Well, you know how I feel about convertibles—"

Mom interrupts. "Petunia."

Now I'm wary. "Yeees. Greatest dog ever. What about her?"

"You got Petunia. You wanted a dog like E wanted her work. Even if you didn't know it at the time." I must look surprised because she adds, "What? You didn't think that your dad and I were softened up by that whole 'it's so hard to adjust to Hollywood' thing, did you?"

Kinda. Yeah.

"Face it, Jess. You'd take that dog over a car any day."

A mom who really knows me . . . and me without my kazoo.

Speaking of making questionable music, the Runny Snots' lead singer is tuning his guitar at the next table.

Can you believe that Murphy came to the party?

Some of the crew are even talking to him! Trying to find out when the *Two Sisters* episode of *Crank Pranksters* will air! So that they can TiVo it!

Seriously? For a moment of airtime, all's forgiven?

Murphy is working the rocker-boy look, with a tighter-than-ever black tee and a new silver lip-piercing. *Ow!* He's traded in the cornrows for a new fashion fault—leather pants.

He gets a rhythm going on the guitar. Am I expecting to be wowed by his talent and performance?

Snot so much.

Life's just another
Prank gone wrong
Rhythm and words
That can't make a song.
You've got the 'chute on

You're ready to fly
Pull the wrong cord
It's do-or-die.
In a love for two
When one don't belong
The game's not more
Than a prank gone wrong.

Yikes. Murphy-lite . . . not what I expected. He catches me watching, and I have to say something. "Did you write that?"

"Not done writing it." When he's not singing, the voice is still pure cabs and crowds.

"Oh, I'm writing a song too."

"Yeah?"

"It's about carpet." Though I don't know if I'll get around to finishing "Red Carpet Burn."

"Uh-huh."

I have to ask. "Why do you do it? Damage things? Set people up?"

His smile shows a lot of teeth. "I set you up, Jess, because you're an easy target. Your bad luck was practically my inspiration. And the rest?" He shrugs. "It was a joke. Get it?" He walks off, whistling.

I remember that Justin Timberlake had to laugh it off when fake federal agents declared him bankrupt and seized his house. "Had to laugh" because the *Punk'd* cameras were rolling.

But I'm not sure that Murphy would know when a joke stops being funny. A part of him flat-out can't resist trouble. Maybe that's why he likes Lavender. The more she treats him like he's a publicity stunt, the more he seems to like her. For real.

Should I devote myself to getting back at Murphy? *Total Revenge Live* and all that?

I watch him walk up to Lavender. Is Murphy going to bring down a world of trouble on himself, with no help from me?

Ah think so.

Then I think about my grandmother.

Abuela has her own way about her. Not crazy—*different*. I was so embarrassed by her talk about kissing that I didn't pay attention to what she was saying. And it was worth listening to: love and attraction are strong forces and you can get swept away by them if you're not careful.

If I hadn't been so worked up about Jeremy, wouldn't I have given him a chance to explain about the kiss with Paige? If he had been a friend, I would have listened. I wouldn't have been so worried about looking pathetic. But since he was my crush, I let my emotions toss me around.

I head over toward my sister. On my way, I pass Carlton hitting on one of the good-looking Wisconsin waitresses. "You'd be perfect for this movie I'm writing. It's an *X-Men* meets *Mary Poppins* story about a team of elite, hot nannies."

Her answer: "Well, that's different." And she keeps moving with her cheese and crackers assortment.

Wisconsin girls . . . polite? Yes. Dumb? No.

I make it to Eva's side just as her stylist friends walk off. "Hey, Jess." She takes a closer look at me. "What's on your mind?"

"Some good advice Abuela gave me."

E stares like maybe I've mixed up the lemonade with the bratwash (that's Wisconsin for beer). "And what was that?"

"Try to be a friend to your boyfriend."

"Sounds suspiciously straightforward for Abuela."

"Well, she may have hidden the meaning a bit," I admit. "So did you get in touch with Keiko? What did the superpublicist have to say about Murphy being a sneak armed with a camera?"

"She texted me four words."

Really?

My guess: "I'm shocked and appalled!" Or "That's so not right!" Maybe: "Dude is seriously twisted."

E flips open her phone so I can read the saved message:

Smile. Till. It. Hurts.

Yowza. "E, what is wrong with the people in your business?"

She looks offended. "*Most* people are more afraid to *look* wrong than be wrong. Except for you, of course."

Really? I can stand for truth against a crowd of lies and misconception? My eyes are misting, ready for a sisterly "you complete me" moment, when she adds, "It doesn't mean you have to fly-tackle every actress who beats me out for a role. Unless you want to."

You complete me . . . then you irritate me.

Which reminds me: "Hey, did you catch Mom giving Jeremy the angry eyes? She usually saves that heat for the twenty-dollar hotel fridge candy."

"Where is that cheating d-a-w-g?" Eva strains to catch sight of Jeremy and Paige at the buffet.

We can hear Paige yelling into her cell. "We all have to work together to make this happen. We're like a mosaic—" Paige stops. Either she was interrupted, or she remembered that she doesn't know what a mosaic is.

How can I explain to E about Jeremy? How could I say that

another person can be like a foreign country? Sometimes things just get lost in translation. "It was a . . . misunderstanding. We're friends again."

"Jess, you were . . ." She doesn't say crying, and I'm grateful. ". . . so upset. You can't press Rewind on that—on how everyone felt to see you like that. Mom and I are going to be mad at Jeremy for a long time."

"And Dad?"

"Angry for *always.*" Eva reaches into her bag and pulls out an iPod. *My* iPod.

"Hey! You borrowed something of mine!"

"Yeah. I did." She flicks it on, and I see a new playlist:

Songs for Getting Over Boys
"You Had Me" by Joss Stone

"Hole in the Head" by the Sugababes

"Fighter" by Christina Aguilera

"I Will Survive" by Gloria Gaynor

"All I Have" by J.Lo

"How You Remind Me" by Nickelback

"These Boots Are Made for Walkin'"
by Nancy Sinatra

"Thanks, E."

"I thought you'd like it, since, you know, you told me you would." I get it. Mysteries are easier to figure out with clues. Even when the mystery is me. "You okay, Jess?"

"As okay as a girl can be when she's not on the dance floor at the hottest party in Wisconsin."

E laughs. "Sounds like the best way to warm up around here."

You never know when brightest happiness might be briefest. Might as well take your fun where you find it, right?

And so we polka. We're not . . . to use tabloid talk . . . "the new hotness." But we're having fun. It's not how Eva and I would have planned it, but that doesn't mean we can't enjoy what we've got—which is a glowing New London sunset, a rocking polka band, and each other.

EXTERIOR SHOT: SUNSET OVER WISCONSIN. CLOSE-UP ON TWO FIGURES DANCING AMID A CROWD. RED AND GOLD PAPER LANTERNS SWAY AGAINST PURPLE SKY.

FADE TO BLACK

ere are three clues to where author Mary Wilcox lives: The movies *Legally Blonde* and *Good Will Hunting* were filmed there. The television show *Sabrina, the Teenage Witch* was set there. Celebrities Uma Thurman, Matt Damon, and Paul Revere were born there.

Visit www.hollywoodsisters.com for more information.

PSST! DON'T MISS THE NEXT BOOK IN
THE *Hollywood Sisters* SERIES

Jeremy. ☺ Alex. ☹ Heathcliff?

Now that we're living in Hollywood, Eva thinks anything is possible—including casting the part of my boyfriend! As for the players: one's an actor (bad sign), one's a snobby rich kid (worse sign), and one doesn't even exist (stop sign). Guess who my sister picked?

And I don't need this distraction—I have a Very Special Guest Star to avoid, tour buses are doing Casa Ortiz drive-bys (and shout-outs), and a cranky prankster is keeping the *Two Sisters* actresses on the tips of their stilettos. Isn't the action supposed to stay *on*-screen?

I go to hide out—*oops*, I mean work on my summer reading—in Eva's dressing room. I'm almost to her door when I hear a familiar voice behind me: "Hey."

"Hey."

My body bypasses my brain and a wave of happy rolls through me. I should not be this glad to talk to Jeremy Jones, but I *am* this glad.

"How are you, Jessica?"

I'm short, dark-haired, and sane, Jeremy, but these days I guess you go for tall, blond, and reality-challenged. I steal a closer look at him: same blue-eyed, *"TeenStyle* Hot List" guy as ever. There are no outward signs of the stress that constant Paige exposure must wreak. "Fine."

"Are you . . . doing that thing you do?"

Flying my bad-luck balloon?

Angering the producer with misread lines?

Wondering what Jeremy is talking about?

The guy is going to have to get a lot more specific about which thing I do.

"How you investigate things? Like the Murphy prank?" Jeremy was a great partner early in the summer when we caught a lighting tech who was stealing from the show, but there's not much of a mystery here now.

"We already know who did it. What's to—" I catch sight of someone over Jeremy's shoulder. "Uh-oh. Hide me."

"What? Is it Murphy? Is he here?"

"No, not him." Okay, when I mentioned that Roman Capo was the *Two Sisters* producer, I forgot to mention his other identity: Jessica Ortiz archenemy. My bad luck has caused such trouble on his sets that today's script screwup doesn't make his top ten list.

Jeremy looks over his shoulder. "I think Roman is waving to you, Jess."

"No, he's not." I try to hide behind Jeremy. "He can't stand me."

"He's got a big smile—"

"Have you forgotten? I'm a natural detective. I know things about people." I make the mistake of peeking over Jeremy's shoulder. My eyes catch Roman's. I'm not turned to stone, but that would probably be a better fate than the usual reaming he gives me.

Jeremy takes my elbow protectively. So he's dragged along when Roman throws out an arm . . . he wouldn't swing at me, would he? *Would he?* . . . and tries for a one-armed hug. "Babe! There you are, sweetheart."

I've ducked out of Roman's armpath so he winds up whapping Jeremy on the back. Roman gives me a huge grin. "Good to see you, kid."

I respond. "Dabba dabba dabba duh?"

Did he pop a contact lens and mistake me for Eva? I am wearing some of her things . . . her shirt, pants, shoes, socks, bracelet, earrings, nail polish.

Jeremy whispers, "Killing you with kindness, huh?"

"Jessica! You always keep it lively!" Roman turns to Jeremy. "Jeremy, the director wants to show you the ladders for that giraffe rescue scene."

"The *Necks Chance* episode? But that's not for another month."

"And yet you're leaving. Now."

Roman bares his teeth at me—um, I mean he smiles—and drags Jeremy away.

Whoa. There are some people who make friendly feel so wrong. Roman Capo? He's definitely in the freaky-friendly camp.

I duck into E's dressing room. Keiko is reading through scripts. "Keiko, does Roman like me all of a sudden?"

"Unlikely."

"But he—"

"I heard it all." Keiko frowns. "Look, Jessica, when it seemed like Jeremy and Paige started dating . . . they got a lot more coverage. The show got more publicity. There will be pressure."

Pressure? "Roman swooped over to keep me away from Jeremy? That's . . . that's insane."

Keiko shakes her head. "No, babe, that's showbiz."

"Don't worry, Jessica!" Eva rushes through the door behind me, with her script still in hand. Could I tear out the page with my poem? E takes my hand and squeezes. "I'm going to take care of everything!"

Eva's last plan for helping me with my love life involved first setting me up with the studio owner's egomaniac son, and when that didn't work out (his kiss was worse than his personality!) she created an imaginary boyfriend for me. She named him "Obviously Made-Up Guy."

Actually, she named him Heathcliff. But, c'mon, it's almost the same thing.

"Don't worry about a thing!" She flashes her famous smile at me.

It's a great smile.

I'd smile back if I didn't know better.

A lot better.